ANNIE

ANNIE

An Old-fashioned Story by

THOMAS MEEHAN

GRANADA
London Toronto Sydney New York

Granada Publishing Limited
Frogmore, St Albans, Herts AL2 2NF
and
36 Golden Square, London W1R 4AH
866 United Nations Plaza, New York, NY 10017, USA
117 York Street, Sydney, NSW 2000, Australia
100 Skyway Avenue, Rexdale, Ontario M9W 3A6, Canada
61 Beach Road, Auckland, New Zealand

Published by Granada Publishing 1982
First published in USA by Macmillan Publishing Co, Inc in 1980

ISBN 0 246 11735 4

Printed in Great Britain by
Richard Clay (The Chaucer Press) Ltd,
Bungay, Suffolk

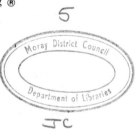

This book is for my children, Kate and Joe

ONE

Long ago. The still and dark early hours of the morning of the first of January, 1933. A light snow was falling in the chill, deserted streets of downtown New York. Time slowly passed, and then the wintry quiet was broken by the clanging of the bells in the steeple of St Mark's in the Bowery, tolling 4.00 am.

A couple of blocks from the church, on St Mark's Place, in the second-floor dormitory of the New York City Municipal Orphanage, Girls' Annex, an eleven-year-old girl stood alone at a frosty window. Shivering in a thin white cotton nightgown, she listened to the tolling of the bells as she watched the snow swirling downward in the light of the street lamp. From time to time, she looked yearningly one way up the street and then the other way down. She was waiting for someone to come for her. To take her away from the orphanage. But no one came. Thin, somewhat short for her age, the girl had a slightly upturned nose and an unruly mop of straightish, short-cut red hair. But her most striking features were shining blue-grey eyes that seemed strangely to reflect at the same time a deep sadness, irrepressible joy, and a sharp intelligence. Her name was Annie.

In the cold, draughty dormitory, the other girls – seventeen of them – had long been asleep, mumbling and occasionally crying out in their dreams as they turned restlessly in narrow beds under scratchy, drab army blankets. But Annie had been awake all night. Earlier, trying to fall asleep, she'd been kept awake by the street sounds of New Year's Eve revellers – shouting voices, drunken singing, the honking of car horns and the raucous blowing of noise-makers. Long after midnight, though, when all had grown quiet on St Mark's Place and the snow had begun to fall, Annie still hadn't been able to sleep. And at last she'd got up from her bed to stand at the window, to keep a silent vigil through the snowy night, to wait.

For as long as she could remember, Annie hadn't been able to sleep on New Year's Eve. Because New Year's Eve marked the anniversary of the night eleven years earlier when she'd been left as a two-month-old baby in a tan wicker basket on the front steps of the orphanage. Someone had rung the doorbell and then run off into the night. Annie had been wrapped in a faded pink woollen blanket and had been wearing a broken half of a silver locket around her neck. And there had been an unsigned note pinned to the blanket. 'Please take good care of our little darling,' the note had read. 'Her name is Annie and we love her very much. She was born on October 28th. We will be back to get her soon. We have left half of a locket around her neck and kept the other half so that when we come back for her you will know that she's our baby.'

Because she'd been left at the orphanage on a New Year's Eve, Annie had got it into her head that somehow her mother and father would come back to get her on a New Year's Eve. So, each year, while other children counted the days until Christmas, Annie instead counted the days until New Year's Eve. But year after year, she'd been disappointed. Her father and mother hadn't come for her. And now it seemed pretty certain that they weren't coming for her this year, either. As the snow began to fall more heavily now, Annie sighed and rubbed her eyes to keep from crying. 'They said they loved me and were comin' back for me – it's in my note,' whispered Annie to herself in the dark. 'What happened? Where are they? Why haven't they come for me?' Annie clasped the broken silver locket that hung around her neck, always, night and day, and squeezed it tightly to her breast.

'Mama, Mama, Mummy!' The littlest of the orphans in the orphanage, six-year-old Molly, had wakened from a nightmare and was crying out for her mother. But Molly's mother had died two years before, in a car accident, and her father had been killed in the same crash. So, although she was an extraordinarily beautiful child, with deep-set dark eyes and long, glistening black hair, Molly was an orphan whom nobody wanted to adopt. An orphan like all of the other girls in the orphanage. Except Annie. Annie was different because *she* had a father and a mother. Somewhere. 'Mama, Mummy!' cried Molly again, waking up the girls in the beds around her.

'Shut up!' shouted Pepper from the next bed.

'Yeah, can't nobody get any sleep around here?' grumbled Duffy.

'Mama, Mummy!' screamed Molly again.

'I said, shut your little trap, Molly,' said Pepper, getting angrily out of bed, picking Molly up, and

9

shoving her down on the floor. At fourteen, Pepper was the oldest and the biggest of the orphans, a pug-nosed rapscallion with a face full of freckles and long, tousled hair that was even redder than Annie's.

'Ahhh, stop pushin' the poor little kid around,' said July. 'She ain't doin' nothin' to you.' Twelve years old, the sweetest of the orphans – if not exactly the prettiest – July had received her name because, simply enough, she'd been abandoned as a baby at the orphanage on the Fourth of July.

'She's keepin' me awake, ain't she?' Pepper snapped back at July.

'No, *you* are keepin' *us* awake,' said July.

'You wanna make somethin' out of it?' said Pepper, walking over to July's bed.

'Oh, the Jack Dempsey of the orphanage,' said July, and in a moment she and Pepper were rolling on the floor in a shrieking, punching, hair-pulling fight that woke up eight-year-old Tessie in her bed at the far end of the dormitory.

'Oh, my goodness, oh, my goodness, they're fightin' and I won't get no sleep at night,' whined Tessie, a pale, frightened girl with blonde pigtails, a thin beaked nose, and scarcely any chin at all. 'Oh, my goodness, oh, my goodness!'

Annie had been silently watching from the window. But now she stepped forward and broke up the fight between Pepper and July. 'C'mon, you two, cut it out and go back to bed,' commanded Annie, pulling the fighting girls apart.

'Aw, nuts to you, Annie,' muttered Pepper, glowering as she stomped back to her bed. But Pepper didn't try to pick a fight with Annie. Although she was a good deal smaller than Pepper, Annie was recognized by all the orphans as the toughest among them. And even Pepper was afraid of her. The smartest of the orphans, too. Annie was their acknowledged leader, especially in their never-ending battles with the headmistress of the orphanage, Miss Agatha Hannigan.

'Pepper started it, Annie,' said July, 'pushin' Molly down.'

'I know,' said Annie, patting July on the shoulder. 'But you gotta go back to sleep, all of you.'

'Okay, Annie,' said July, climbing back into her bed as Annie went now to comfort little Molly who was still crouched on the floor. Kneeling beside Molly, Annie pulled the child into her arms.

'It's all right, Molly, Annie's here,' said Annie, gently stroking Molly's long, black hair.

'It was my mama, Annie,' said Molly, tears streaming down her flushed cheeks. 'We was ridin' on the ferryboat and she was holdin' me up to see the big ships. And then she was walkin' away, wavin', and I couldn't find her no more. Anywhere.'

'It was only a dream, honey,' said Annie, drying Molly's eyes with the sleeve of her nightgown. 'Now, you gotta get back to sleep. It's after four o'clock.'

'Annie,' said Molly, 'read me your note.'

'Again?' said Annie.

'*Please*,' said Molly.

'Okay, Molly,' said Annie, and from the battered wicker basket under her bed – the same basket in which she'd been left at the orphanage and in which she kept her few belongings – Annie took out the note and started

11

to read it aloud by the pale light that slanted in from the street lamp outside. Annie had folded and unfolded the note so many times that it was nearly falling apart. It was written in a round, feminine hand on a square of pale-blue cardboard. 'Please take good care of our little darling,' Annie began. 'Her name is . . .'

'Oh, no, here it comes again,' groaned Pepper. In the years that they'd all been together in the orphanage, Annie had read her note aloud to the orphans on an average of perhaps two or three times a week. 'Her name is Annie,' said Duffy in a mocking, singsong voice. A tubby thirteen-year-old with a pudding face and scraggly blonde hair, Duffy was Pepper's best friend. 'She was born on October twenty-eighth,' Duffy went on. 'We will be back to get her soon.' And now all the orphans began laughing at Duffy's rendition of the note. All, that is, but Molly and Tessie. 'Oh, my goodness, now they're laughin' and I won't get no sleep at night,' whined Tessie. 'Oh, my goodness, oh, my goodness.'

Annie angrily stood up, put her hands on her hips, and faced the laughing girls. 'All right,' said Annie, 'do you wanna sleep with your teeth inside your mouth or out?' Silence. Everyone, including Pepper, lay quietly back down in bed. Annie finished reading the note and then, folding it with great care, put it back in her basket. Now, Annie picked Molly up and carried her to bed. She tucked the little girl in under the covers and kissed her lightly on the forehead.

'Good night, Molly,' whispered Annie.

'Good night, Annie,' said Molly. 'You're lucky, Annie, I dream about havin' a mother and father. But you really got 'em.'

'I know,' said Annie softly. 'Somewhere. Somewhere.' In a few minutes, Molly and the other orphans had fallen back to sleep. But Annie still couldn't sleep. And she went again to the window to look out on the falling snow. At the window, she drifted into a waking dream about her father and mother. They were maybe real nearby, she thought, or maybe far away. Her father, she knew, was a big, strapping man who laughed and smiled all the time, and who'd pick her up in his arms, give her a big bear hug, and whirl her about the room. He was a lawyer, or maybe even a doctor, who helped poor people. And her mother was a kind, gentle woman with golden-blonde hair who played songs on the piano and sewed even better than a professional dressmaker. She'd made dozens of beautiful dresses for Annie. The dresses, all the colours of the rainbow, were hanging in a closet waiting for the day when Annie came home. Annie and her parents lived in the country, in a vine-covered house on a hill. There was a broad front lawn, and from the porch you could see for miles across green meadows to a distant winding river. On summer afternoons, Annie, her mother, and her father, the three of them together, would walk across the meadows to the river and have a picnic of devilled eggs and lemonade while they watched swans gliding by. In her room in the house, Annie had a canopy bed and a three-storey dollhouse and a red-and-white hobbyhorse and . . . A horse-drawn milk wagon came clattering around the corner of St Mark's Place, waking Annie with a start from her reverie. She'd heard the sound of the milk wagon outside the window in the early morning ever since she could remember. Annie began thinking back now on all of her long years in the orphanage. And almost none of her memories of those years were happy ones.

TWO

Annie's earliest memory, from a time when she was perhaps two or three years old, was of the shadowy figure of Miss Hannigan looming menacingly above her as she played with a tattered rag doll on the floor of the dormitory. 'Get up from there, you wretched little orphan – you've got that clean dress all filthy!' shrieked Miss Hannigan, a skinny, hatchet-faced woman with short, jet-black hair. She reminded the orphans of a particularly unpleasant-looking – and all too real – Halloween witch. Miss Hannigan had yanked Annie to her feet and given her a dozen whacks across the backside with a heavy oaken paddle. But Annie hadn't cried. Even as a tiny tot, Annie had never cried when Miss Hannigan beat her, a show of spirit that infuriated Miss Hannigan.

Because Annie was at once the spunkiest and the most intelligent of the girls in the orphanage, Miss Hannigan hated her more than any child she'd had under her charge in all her twenty-three years as headmistress of the orphanage. 'I'll break that little brat yet,' muttered Miss Hannigan to herself, and she constantly gave Annie extra chores to do – greasy pots and pans to wash in the orphanage's steamy basement kitchen, grimy windows to wash, floors to scrub on her hands and knees. But Annie never let her spirits flag and made

Miss Hannigan all the angrier by taking on each new task with a cheery smile – the worse the chore, the broader Annie's smile. 'You see, it's me against Miss Hannigan, like a war,' Annie told the other orphans, 'and I'm not gonna give in to her, ever.'

As the years passed, Annie grew accustomed to the routine of life in the orphanage. Each morning, at 6.00 a.m., the piercing shrill of Miss Hannigan's police whistle woke the slumbering orphans. 'All right, get up, get up, all of you, you rotten orphans!' shouted Miss Hannigan. A cold shower, and then the girls dressed themselves in hand-me-downs that came twice a year in large bundles from the Salvation Army. Their beds made and the dormitory swept, the orphans were marched downstairs to the first-floor dining room for breakfast. 'No talking!' snapped Miss Hannigan. The girls sat silently on hard wooden benches at a long trestle table as Miss Hannigan served up breakfast. For as far back as Annie could remember, breakfast in the orphanage had always been the same – a glass of bluish skim milk and a bowl of hot mush. The mush, which was prepared by Miss Hannigan herself, was mouse-grey in colour and lumpy in texture, and it tasted the way that white school paste smelled. When they'd first come to the orphanage, many of the girls had gagged on Miss Hannigan's mush and hadn't been able to swallow so much as a spoonful. But, after a time, they'd grown used to it. Because, for breakfast, in the orphanage, it was either mush or nothing.

After breakfast, the schedule in the orphanage varied according to whether or not it was a school day. If there was school, Miss Hannigan marched the orphans down

16

the block to PS 62, a turreted Victorian red brick public school at the corner of St Mark's Place and Third Avenue. The orphans stayed in school until four o'clock, when Miss Hannigan picked them up and herded them back to the orphanage. If there was no school, the orphans went downstairs immediately after breakfast to their basement workroom, where they sat at rows of sewing machines making little girls' dresses. On their working days, the orphans sewed for eight hours, with twenty minutes out for lunch (another glass of skim milk and a sandwich of fatty ham or bologna). Each girl was expected by the end of the day to have finished at least one dress. Or else she got the paddle from Miss Hannigan. The dresses that they made – frilly party frocks of organdie and chiffon in such bright colours as canary-yellow or magenta – were in marked contrast to the drab and patched hand-me-downs that they wore. Miss Hannigan had arranged for a children's clothing manufacturer in Brooklyn to provide the sewing machines and the raw fabrics in exchange for being able to buy the finished dresses for fifty cents apiece. Most weeks Miss Hannigan made as much as thirty dollars for herself out of the orphans' labours. The orphans weren't supposed to work, of course, and if the director of the New York City Board of Orphans, Mr Joseph Donatelli, had known what Miss Hannigan was up to, he would quickly have fired her. But no one had come from the Board of Orphans to inspect the girls' annex on St Mark's Place for more than a dozen years. And Miss Hannigan justified what she was doing by telling herself that she was teaching the orphans a useful trade. 'You oughta be grateful to me, you little brats – you'll be able to get a job sewin' when you grow up and gotta leave here,' Miss Hannigan told the orphans as they bent hour after hour over their sewing machines in the dank basement workshop.

Miss Hannigan spent most of the money that she made from selling the dresses on bottles of bootleg whiskey. For Miss Hannigan was a heavy drinker who was slightly drunk from morning until night – while the orphans were either working at their sewing machines or off at school, Miss Hannigan idled away most of her days in her high-ceilinged office sipping rye whiskey, smoking Lucky Strike cigarettes, and listening to soap operas like 'Ma Perkins' and 'The Romance of Helen Trent' on her table-model Philco radio.

At six o'clock each evening, the orphans filed into the dining room for supper, a meal that most often consisted of boiled chicken wings, greyish boiled potatoes, and some such soggy vegetable as boiled cabbage or broccoli. There was spongy white bread and margarine to fill up on, but dessert was served only on special occasions like Thanksgiving or Christmas, when each orphan got a bowl of gummy rice pudding. After supper, the orphans were sent upstairs to their dormitory for a period of study until bedtime. Lights out at eight o'clock, and another day in the orphanage was done.

Sunday was the only day of rest for the orphans. But, in a way, Sunday was the worst day of all for them. Miss Hannigan led the girls to St Mark's in the Bowery each Sunday morning at eight o'clock, and they sat for more than an hour in the musty church listening to long-winded sermons about the ultimate fate of all who

18

sinned – the eternal fires of hell. And, of course, as Miss Hannigan explained to them, an orphaned girl was by nature a sinner. Or why else would her mother and father have died on her? Racked by confused feelings of guilt, fear, and boredom, the orphans were paraded from the church back to the orphange, where Miss Hannigan made them spend the day praying and reflecting on the evil they had done in the past week. 'Cleanse your filthy souls with remorse and beg God for forgiveness for your multitude of sins!' thundered Miss Hannigan at the frightened orphans. No talking. No reading. Only sitting silently with bowed heads and folded hands for endless hours at the trestle table in the airless dining room. There were Sunday afternoons in the orphanage, Annie remembered now as she stood at the window looking out on the falling snow, that had seemed to last forever.

School days were happier for Annie than the days spent at her sewing machine. But not much happier. Still, at school she had a chance to read, which was her favourite pastime. Annie eagerly read her way through scores of books each year. The books she loved best, like *The Five Little Peppers*, were about poor but happy children and cheerful families. And she also loved adventure books that were set in romantic, faraway places, like the South Sea islands. Annie did well in school, getting good marks in every subject and ranking near the top of her class. But the orphans, including Annie, were constantly teased and ridiculed by the other schoolchildren, because of their raggedy clothes and because they didn't have mothers, fathers, or homes of their own. As they were herded to and from school by

Miss Hannigan, the orphans were often mocked by the other children, who taunted them with a crude rhyme they'd invented:

> Orphan, orphan, ha, ha, ha,
> Ain't got a mama, ain't got a pa,
> Orphan, orphan, dumb, dumb, dumb,
> Lookin' like a pig, dressed like a bum!

In winter, the other children sometimes made a game out of seeing how many orphans they could hit with snowballs. And Miss Hannigan didn't allow the orphans to step out of line to throw snowballs back. Teeth clenched, eyes forward, the orphans trudged two by two along the slushy city sidewalk through a gauntlet of cruelly laughing children and flying snowballs.

The teachers at PS 62 weren't especially kind to the orphans, either. In each class, the orphans were assigned to a special section of desks at the back of the room and treated by their teachers as pesky nuisances who didn't really belong in school. Annie remembered having overheard her fifth-grade teacher, Mrs Conklin, talking one day to another teacher. 'Damned orphans, cluttering up our classrooms,' Mrs Conklin had complained. 'Without them our job would be a cinch.'

At lunchtime, as though they had some terrible disease that the other children might catch, the orphans were put in a special corner section of the school cafeteria. They ate some such sodden glop as baked macaroni and cheese that was provided free to needy students by the New York City Board of Education, while the rest of the children, who'd brought their lunches in shiny metal lunchboxes, had meals that their mothers had fixed for them – mysterious and wonderful things that the orphans yearningly dreamed of tasting, like peanut-butter-and-jelly sandwiches, bananas, chocolate brownies, and hot cocoa poured from Thermos bottles.

During the half-hour morning and afternoon recess periods, in the fenced-in concrete playground behind the school, the orphans, left out of the other children's games, banded together to play games of their own. And to protect themselves against the playground bullies, who from time to time decided that it would be fun to beat up an orphan. Against these bullies, the orphans, led by Annie and Pepper, put up a united front. 'You touch any one of us,' said Annie fiercely, 'and all of us will jump you!' At home, in the orphanage, the orphans often fought and bickered with one another, but at school they stuck loyally together. And the bullies at PS 62 soon learned that it didn't pay to take on the orphans, unless they were looking for a couple of black eyes. They particularly learned not to get mixed up in a fight with Annie, who could flatten even the biggest and the toughest-looking of the boys with a single punch. So, after a while, the orphans were left alone during recess to play their own games of tag or hopscotch.

After reading, Annie's favourite subject was geography. She loved learning about parts of the world that were as totally different and as far distant as possible from PS 62, the orphanage, and St Mark's Place. The country that she loved studying about most of all was Switzerland, with its sparkling-clear lakes and green meadows, and towering snow-capped mountains. She often day-dreamed that her father and mother would turn out to be living in Switzerland and that she'd soon be going to stay with them, forever, in a mountainside Swiss chalet, like a little girl named Heidi whom she'd read about in a book. But as she thought now at the window about geography, Annie remembered something that had happened the previous year at school, when she'd been in the fifth grade. It was one of the most painful memories of her life.

THREE

One Monday morning in early May, her teacher, Mrs Conklin, had arrived in class with a beautifully illustrated 375-page Rand-McNally *Atlas of the World*. The atlas, Mrs Conklin announced, would be awarded on the final day of school, June 23rd, to the fifth-grade pupil who won a special geography spelling bee to be held on the morning of that day. The students, said Mrs Conklin, would be expected to name and to spell correctly all forty-eight states of the United States as well as their capital cities. 'For example,' said Mrs Conklin, a grey-haired, stern-faced woman who wore steel-rimmed spectacles, 'the first state of the union, in alphabetical order, is Alabama, capital A-l-a-b-a-m-a, Alabama, and its capital is Montgomery, capital M-o-n-t-g-o-m-e-r-y, Montgomery. One spelling mistake and a pupil will be eliminated from the spelling bee. We will continue until only one pupil is left, and he or she will be the winner of the atlas.'

Suddenly, Annie wanted more than anything else in the world to win the Rand-McNally atlas. For it struck her that if her mother and father didn't come for her soon, she might have to go out into the world to look for them. And she could use the atlas, with its coloured maps of all the states and every country on earth, to help her find them. Annie didn't know exactly how the atlas could help her find her parents, but it would surely, she felt, in some magical way, lead her to them. And so, in the weeks that followed, Annie spent every moment she could spare learning the names of the states and their capitals and memorizing their spellings. At the orphanage, in the period each evening between supper and bedtime, she'd have her best pal, Kate, who was nine, sit with a geography book and read off the states to her. 'Mississippi,' Kate would say. 'Mississippi, capital M-i-double-s-i-double-s-i-double-p-i, Mississippi,' Annie would reply. 'And the capital of Mississippi is Jackson, capital J-a-c-k-s-o-n, Jackson.' On and on Annie and Kate would go until they'd gotten through all forty-eight states. All the orphans were rooting for Annie to win the atlas. Except Pepper. 'For crumb's sake, Annie, you're drivin' us nuts with all of that spellin' every night,' Pepper grumbled. 'Who cares whether you win any dumb atlas or not?' But Annie ignored Pepper. After lights-out, lying in her narrow bed, she kept on spelling to herself, finally dozing off at around ten o'clock while she tried to remember, for example, how to spell the capital of Florida, Talahasee, or was it Tallahasee? Talla-hassee?

The day of the spelling bee at last arrived. Annie marched off to PS 62 with the other orphans that morning, confident that there wasn't a state or a capital city in the United States that she didn't know how to spell. As Annie figured it, her main competitors in the spelling contest would be Philip Bissell, a pale, puny bookworm and the smartest boy in the class, and Myrtle Vandenmeer. Green-eyed and blonde, with an upturned

24

nose and glittery braces on her teeth, Myrtle was the richest and smartest girl in Annie's class. Her father was a dentist who everybody said made twelve thousand dollars a year! Myrtle lived with her parents on St Mark's Place in a four-storey brownstone house that they had all to themselves. Myrtle had her own bedroom in the house as well as a top-floor playroom filled with dolls and dollhouses and a stuffed life-size lamb from France. She wore expensive dresses which her mother bought for her at Best's, on Fifth Avenue, and she went on vacations with her parents each summer to someplace called Cape Cod. Myrtle was the leader of a pack of fifth-grade girls whose favourite sport was making fun of the orphans. Making fun especially of Annie.

The greatest source of humiliation for Annie at school was the fact that she was the only child who didn't have a last name. Even the other orphans, like Pepper and Molly and Duffy, had arrived at the orphanage with last names of their own, but there had been no mention of a last name in Annie's note. So, to her vast embarrassment, Annie was known both at the orphanage and at school simply as Annie Orphan. From their earliest days in school together, when they'd had Miss Kniss for kindergarten, Myrtle had made fun of Annie for having no last name. 'Oh, look who's here – Annie Orphan,' Myrtle would say with a giggle to her friends. 'Orphan Annie, Little Orphan Annie, hasn't got no Mammy!' If Annie ran after her, Myrtle would go crying to Miss Kniss, saying, 'Teacher, teacher, Annie Orphan tried to hit me again!' And as often as not, it was Annie who would end up in trouble, sent to

25

the principal's office and made to do hours of extra homework because she'd 'bullied' Myrtle. Meanwhile, Myrtle, who behaved like a perfect little blonde angel whenever any of the teachers were around, reigned each year as teacher's pet. If I'm going to lose the spelling bee to anybody, thought Annie that morning, please, God, don't let it be Myrtle Vandenmeer.

The spelling bee went just about the way that Annie had figured it would. The dimmer-witted children in the class were quickly eliminated, stumbling on the spelling of states like Missouri or capital cities like Sacramento, and within a few minutes only five students were left in the spelling bee – Tommy Warbrick, Margaret McManiss, Philip Bissell, Myrtle, and Annie. In the third round, Tommy lost out when he misspelled Frankfort, Kentucky, and Margaret soon followed him by forgetting that the capital of New Hampshire is Concord. For a long time, as Annie dug her nails into her palms to contain her nervousness and excitement, each of the three remaining contestants – Philip, Myrtle, and Annie – went on without making a mistake, correctly spelling such tough states as Mississippi and capitals as Annapolis. But then Philip misspelled Montpelier, Vermont, and suddenly only Myrtle and Annie were left in the contest.

The two girls stood alone at the front of the classroom as Mrs Conklin, with a geography book opened before her, sat at her desk calling out names in a false, ringing voice. It seemed to Annie that she was given the more difficult states to spell, like Minnesota and Massachusetts, while Myrtle was given states like Texas and Ohio.

26

But neither girl made a mistake as state after state went by, and it began to look as if the spelling bee might end up in a two-way tie. But then Myrtle was given Florida. 'Florida, capital F-l-o-r-i-d-a, Florida,' enunciated Myrtle in her sing-song, stuck-up voice, clearly confident that she was going to win the contest. 'And the capital of Florida is Tallahassee, capital T-a-l-l-a-h-a-s-e-e, Tallahassee.'

Mrs Conklin's pale face suddenly turned red with fury, for she now had to face the unarguable fact that Myrtle – the brilliant, rich Myrtle Vandenmeer – had misspelled Tallahassee. 'I'm sorry, Myrtle, but that is incorrect,' said Mrs Conklin through gritted teeth. 'You are eliminated and you may return to your seat.' Myrtle stared at the teacher with utter disbelief, and then rage took over. 'It isn't fair, it isn't fair, Annie cheated!' snarled Myrtle, stomping angrily back to her seat and kicking her chair with her expensive little Mary Jane shoes before sitting down.

Now, her heart pounding with unaccustomed joy, Annie stood alone at the front of the class. 'Does this mean I win?' she asked Mrs Conklin. 'No, you do not win unless you can correctly spell the capital city that Myrtle was unable to spell,' said Mrs Conklin after a moment of hesitation. She'd quickly changed the rules in the hope that the contest might at least end up in a tie between Myrtle and Annie. 'Spell Tallahassee.'

Annie closed her eyes and tried to remember how the city had been spelled in her geography book. It had always been the most difficult one of all for her to remember. 'Tallahassee,' said Annie, 'capital T-a-l-l-a-

h-a' – she paused for a moment and took a deep breath –
's-s-e-e, Tallahassee.' Mrs Conklin glared at Annie with
undisguised hatred in her cold, slate-blue eyes.
'Correct,' she said with difficulty. Annie broke out
in an enormous grin – this was the best she'd ever
felt under the roof of PS 62 – as her fellow
orphans in the class, including even Pepper and
Duffy, let out whoops of delight. 'Silence!' snapped
Mrs Conklin.

'Do I get my atlas now?' Annie asked.

'No, the atlas will be awarded during the All-School
Assembly,' said Mrs Conklin. 'Now return to your
place.' Annie walked in a daze of triumph to her seat at
the back of the room, passing Myrtle, who hissed,
'Dumb orphan, you were just lucky.' But Annie didn't
care now what mean things Myrtle had to say to her –
she'd won the Rand-McNally atlas!

Every year, on the last day of school at PS 62,
parents were invited to an All-School Assembly in the
auditorium, where awards were handed out to pupils
who'd won special honours. This year every seat in the
auditorium was taken, and in the first row, haughtily
arranging themselves in their seats, sat Myrtle's father
and mother, Dr and Mrs Vandenmeer. Up on the stage,
the school's principal, Mr Drennan, led everyone in
the Pledge of Allegiance to the Flag, the sixth-grade
chorus sweetly sang 'America, the Beautiful', off key,
and then the passing out of the awards began. Her heart
racing a million miles a second, Annie could hardly wait
for her turn to go up on the stage to receive her award.
More than a dozen books and certificates and medals
were handed out before Mr Drennen called on Mrs

Conklin to present the fifth-grade geography spelling bee award. Mrs Conklin bustled onto the stage and stepped to the speakers' podium, carrying the Rand-McNally atlas, its glossy cover seeming to Annie almost to shine. 'The winner of the fifth-grade geography spelling bee,' called out Mrs Conklin in a loud, official voice, 'who receives this handsome Rand-McNally atlas for her achievement, is . . . Myrtle Vandenmeer.'

Annie sat stunned with disbelief – she felt as if she'd been hit very hard in the stomach – as the parents loudly applauded and Myrtle marched mincingly up onto the stage from her seat to get the award. Suddenly, Pepper was standing on her feet in the middle of the auditorium. 'Hey, that ain't fair, Myrtle didn't win the spelling bee, Annie did!' shouted Pepper. 'Silence that child!' called out Mr Drennen, and a pair of teachers quickly collared Pepper and dragged her out of the auditorium as she still shouted, 'It ain't fair, it ain't fair!' Annie herself sat quietly, swallowing, gritting her teeth, looking upward, but not crying – she wouldn't give Myrtle or Mrs Conklin the satisfaction of seeing her burst into tears. But inside she thought her heart would break as she watched Myrtle come down from the stage with the atlas and go to her beaming parents to be kissed and hugged.

When the assembly was over, Annie walked up to Mrs Conklin by the water fountain in the hallway. 'Mrs Conklin, that wasn't fair – you know that I won the spelling bee and should've gotten the atlas,' said Annie. She knew that if she got angry it would be easier not to cry. Mrs Conklin looked icily down at her. 'Orphans are not eligible to receive awards on occasions when parents are in attendance,' declared Mrs Conklin, turning on her heel and walking away. And then Myrtle Vandenmeer strolled by, between her parents, with the Rand-McNally atlas clutched in her arms. 'Nah, nah, nah, dumb orphan,' said Myrtle, sticking out her tongue at Annie. Annie said nothing.

Later, Annie remembered the day that she didn't get the atlas as maybe the saddest and most bitter of her entire life up to then. But most of her other memories were sad, too. At the window, she thought now about the Christmas that had just passed. A few days before Christmas, little Molly had stepped up to Miss Hannigan and asked, 'Miss Hannigan, is there a Santa Claus?' Miss Hannigan had glowered at Molly for a moment, and then she'd smiled and gently replied, 'Yes, dear, of course there's a Santa Claus.' Molly's face broke into a happy smile. 'But,' added Miss Hannigan with a cruel, cackling laugh, 'he don't come to no rotten little orphans like you!' 'Oh,' said Molly, 'then what are we gonna get for Christmas?' 'What did you get last year?' asked Miss Hannigan. 'Nothin',' said Molly. 'Well, you're gettin' it again,' cackled Miss Hannigan.

And indeed the girls in the orphanage had once again this year received no Christmas presents other than what they'd given to one another. On Christmas morning, for example, Annie had given Kate a wire hanger that she'd bent into the outline of a Christmas angel, and Pepper had given Molly a pocket comb. 'Gee, thanks, Pepper, an Ace comb, that's the best kind, with only two teeth missing,' Molly said gratefully. 'Hey, let me see that comb, that's mine!' screamed Duffy. 'You dirty rat, Pepper, you swiped it from me!' 'Ahh, shut your trap, Duffy,' snarled Pepper, and the two girls had got into a hair-pulling fight. Later, Molly had offered to give back the stolen comb, but Duffy had shrugged and told her to keep it. 'That's okay, kid, it's your Christmas present – from me . . . and Pepper,' said Duffy. And so another Christmas had passed at the orphanage without a tree, store-bought presents, or a visit from Santa Claus.

Annie suddenly realized that she'd been standing all night at the window. As the snow continued to fall, a faint light was beginning to show in the sky above St Mark's Place. It was the first day of the new year, 1933, a time when most people were looking ahead with hope to the coming months. But Annie had nothing to look ahead to but a continued life of drudgery under the iron fist of Miss Hannigan. When she reached the age of sixteen, Annie would be released from the orphanage to go out into the world on her own. But she wouldn't be sixteen for another five years. Five more years in the orphanage. Annie thought about something Pepper had said a few days earlier when she'd been talking about how her parents would soon be coming to take her home. 'You dumb cluck,' said Pepper, 'your parents are never comin' for you.' And Annie knew now that Pepper had been right. If her father and mother hadn't turned up at the orphanage after all these years, she had to face the fact that they weren't ever coming for her. Not ever. And so she'd have to go and find *them*. 'That's it,' whispered Annie determinedly to herself, 'I've

got to go and find them, get out of here – run away.'
Yes, she decided, I'm going to run away! When? Right
now!

FOUR

Annie tiptoed from her place at the window back to her bed, and in the pale light of dawn, she quickly got out of her nightgown and dressed as warmly as she could for the chill day that awaited her outside the orphanage. She didn't have a winter coat of course, and she'd have to make do with the raggedy maroon wool sweater that she wore each day to school. She took her wicker basket from under her bed and hastily filled it with her meagre belongings – some underwear, socks, and an extra dress. She made sure that she had her locket and her note and then, picking up the basket, turned to go. But, in her haste, she banged the basket against her iron bedstead, and the clanging sound awoke several of the girls in the beds near her.

'Now what?' groaned Pepper.

'Annie, whatta you doin'?' asked Kate.

'Runnin' away,' said Annie.

'Oh, my goodness!' cried Tessie.

'I just know now that my folks are never comin' for me,' said Annie, her basket on her arm, poised to leave. 'So I gotta go find them.'

'Annie, you're crazy,' said July. 'Miss Hannigan'll catch you.'

'And give you the paddle,' warned Tessie.

'I don't care, I'm gettin' out of here,' Annie said.

33

'And I'm ready. Goin' now. Wish me luck.'

All the orphans but Pepper, who was shaking her head in disgust, quietly whispered good-bye. 'Good luck, Annie!' 'We'll miss you, Annie.' Looking back, Annie saw that Molly was sitting up in bed, her head bowed and her large dark eyes abrim with tears. Annie went to Molly and embraced her. 'Good-bye, Molly,' said Annie gently, hugging Molly to her. 'When I find my folks, I'll come back for you, and we'll live together, all of us, you and me and my folks.'

'You promise, Annie?' asked Molly.

'I promise.'

'Okay, Annie,' said Molly. 'Good-bye, Annie. I love you.'

As the other girls knelt on their beds and watched her go, Annie tiptoed to the top of the stairs that led from the dormitory down to the front hallway. She listened for Miss Hannigan. All was quiet downstairs in the orphanage. 'Okay, here I go,' said Annie with a last wave to her friends. 'So long, dumbbell,' whispered Pepper. 'And good luck.'

The stairs creaked as Annie went slowly down on tiptoe, one step at a time. It seemed to Annie as though it were taking her hours to get down just one flight of stairs. Somewhere outside a car horn honked. Now she was at last at the bottom of the stairs. The big oaken front door that led to freedom – and maybe to her father and mother – was only four steps away. One step. Two steps. Three steps. She reached out to turn the front doorknob.

'Aha, caught ya!' shrieked Miss Hannigan, leaping

out from under the staircase, grabbing Annie by the scruff of her neck and flinging her violently to the floor. 'I heard ya, ya rotten orphan, I *always* hear ya! Now, get up. Get up!'

'Yes, Miss Hannigan,' said Annie, getting warily to her feet. She saw that Miss Hannigan, in a ratty-looking peach-coloured flannel bathrobe, was brandishing the heavy oaken paddle with which she regularly smacked the orphans.

Annie and Miss Hannigan glared at each other. 'Turn around,' commanded Miss Hannigan, but Annie didn't move. 'I said, turn around!' Miss Hannigan shouted. As slowly as she could, Annie turned around, and Miss Hannigan whacked her a dozen painful times across the backside with the heavy paddle. But Annie neither cried out nor even flinched – her stern pride and her hatred of Miss Hannigan had made her all but numb over the years to the beatings she took.

'There!' said Miss Hannigan, breathing heavily from her labours. Her breath reeked of rye whiskey. 'Now, what do you say?'

Annie said nothing, even though she knew what she was supposed to say – the phrase that Miss Hannigan made the orphans greet her with each morning.

'*What . . . do . . . you . . . say?*' repeated Miss Hannigan.

'*I . . . love . . . you . . . Miss Hannigan,*' said Annie through gritted teeth.

'Rotten orphan!' snarled Miss Hannigan.

'I'm not a rotten orphan!' Annie shouted, 'My mother and father left a note sayin' they loved me and they were coming back for me!'

'Yeah, that was in 1922,' said Miss Hannigan with a cruel laugh, ' and this is 1933. Now, take them damn things and get back upstairs.'

'Yes, Miss Hannigan.' Annie picked up her basket and trudged defeatedly back up to the dormitory, where the other orphans, who'd heard everything that had gone on below, were hiding under their blankets. Alone at the bottom of the stairs, Miss Hannigan took a long swig of whiskey from the bottle in her bathrobe pocket and followed Annie up the stairs. Storming into the dormitory, Miss Hannigan flicked on the lights, blew the police whistle that always hung around her neck, and screamed at the children, 'You in here – get up, get up!'

'Yes, Miss Hannigan,' said the orphans, sighing as they got up and went to stand in a row at the foot of their beds. They shivered in their thin cotton nightgowns and bare feet on the cold wooden floor.

'All right, for this one's shenanigans,' said Miss Hannigan, pointing a bony finger at Annie, 'you'll stay up and scrub this floor.'

'But it's five o'clock in the morning,' whined Tessie.

'I know,' said Miss Hannigan with a mean laugh. 'And you'll get down on your knobby little knees and clean this dump until it shines like the top of the Chrysler Building. Get to work!'

'Yes, Miss Hannigan,' said the orphans. Shoulders slumped they filed to the corner closet to get out the buckets and scrub brushes with which they cleaned the dormitory floor several times a week.

'Why any kid would want to be an orphan I'll never know,' muttered Miss Hannigan to herself as she went downstairs to begin cooking the mush for the orphans' breakfast.

'Gee, I'm sorry, kids,' said Annie, as the orphans lined up in the washroom to fill their buckets from the tap in the sink.

'Yeah, sorry, a lotta good that does us,' grumbled Pepper. 'You and your dumb ideas, runnin' away, gettin' us all in Dutch.'

'It's okay, it ain't your fault, Annie,' Kate said.

'And, heck, you're still here,' said Molly with a happy grin. 'So I don't mind scrubbin' no floor.'

'Thanks, Molly,' Annie said. 'And hey, kids, Happy New Year!'

'Huh, some Happy New Year,' muttered Pepper, as the orphans got down on their hands and knees and began the dreary job of scrubbing the cold dormitory floor.

'Rotten smelly life,' said Duffy.

As the orphans worked, the snow stopped falling outside and a pale winter sun came up over St Mark's Place. Day dawned, and a new year had begun in the orphanage. Scrubbing away on her hands and knees, Annie agreed with the complaints of the other orphans. It was true – they lived a cheerless life that stretched before them like an endless prison sentence. And Annie became more determined than ever to run away from the orphanage. She might have failed in her first attempt to get away, but she wasn't going to fail in her next one. 'I'm gettin' outta here,' Annie said to herself. 'I am, I am, as soon as I spot the chance.'

And Annie spotted her chance two mornings later, just before Miss Hannigan was to march the orphans off to school, when the laundry man, a plump, lumbering dimwit named Bundles McCloskey, showed up at the orphanage. 'Mornin', kids, clean sheets once a month whether ya need 'em or not,' chuckled Bundles, lugging in a huge bundle of clean linens from the laundry truck he'd parked outside the front door of the orphanage. Whenever Bundles delivered clean laundry, the orphans were expected to strip their beds and put their dirty sheets and pillowcases into a large laundry bag for Bundles to tote away. As they began pulling off the sheets, Annie suddenly had an idea. Quickly, she told the other orphans what she had in mind – she'd get into the bag with the dirty laundry, and then Pepper and Duffy would carry it out and put it in the back of the truck for Bundles. Downstairs, in the front hallway, Bundles was gabbing with Miss Hannigan, and this gave Annie plenty of time to get into her sweater and to climb into the laundry bag with her wicker basket of belongings. Pepper and Duffy hefted the unwieldy bag and toted it down to the front hallway.

'We'll put the bag in your truck for you, Bundles,' offered Pepper.

'Okay, thanks, kids,' said Bundles.

'Oh, no, you don't,' Miss Hannigan growled. 'You're not here to do his work for him. Now, get outta here with that damn laundry, Bundles.'

'Okay, gorgeous, have it your way,' said Bundles good-naturally, heaving the laundry bag, with Annie, in it, up onto his shoulder. 'Whew,' he said, 'either I'm gettin' weak in my old age or this here laundry of yours is gettin' heavier every month.' Thank goodness

38

Bundles is such a dumb cluck, thought Annie inside the laundry bag, trying not to move as her heart pounded with fear and excitement. Miss Hannigan wasn't stupid, of course, and at any moment, Annie knew, she might figure out what was going on and try to stop Bundles. Annie could hear Pepper saying, 'Here, we'll at least open the door for you,' and then she felt a sudden draught of cold air as Bundles went down the front stoop and out to his truck. She felt herself and the bag being thrown into the back of the truck, and she heard the back door of the truck slamming shut behind her. So far, so good. At least she'd made it safely out of the orphanage and into the truck right under the nose of Miss Hannigan! Annie held her breath and prayed as she heard Bundles trying to get his old truck started in the cold of the January morning. The engine coughed and groaned but didn't start. And then, with a sinking heart, Annie heard Miss Hannigan shouting from the doorway, 'Bundles, Bundles, stop, don't go!' Clearly, Miss Hannigan had discovered that she was missing, thought Annie, and had figured out that she was in the laundry bag. Annie heard Miss Hannigan's footsteps coming down the front steps and up to the laundry truck. 'You stupid oaf, you didn't give me a receipt for that dirty laundry you took,' said Miss Hannigan to Bundles. 'Oh, yeah, sorry, Aggie,' said Bundles, and after a moment Annie could hear Miss Hannigan's footsteps going back up the front stoop of the orphanage as Bundles again attempted to start the truck. 'Whew,' said Annie to herself, 'I thought she was comin' for me for sure.' All of a sudden, Bundles' motor started with a loud clatter, and the truck went rattling off down the street. Annie had escaped!

A few minutes later, in the orphanage, Miss Hannigan was lining up the girls for their march to school and counting them off, prison style, as she did each morning, to make sure that all were on hand. 'Fourteen, fifteen, sixteen . . .' counted Miss Hannigan. 'Wait a minute, Annie . . . where's that Annie?'

Replied the orphans in a chorus of sweet, angelic voices, 'Annie ain't here, Miss Hannigan.'

'Whatta ya mean, "Annie ain't here"?'

'She went,' said Pepper, 'with Mr Bundles.'

'In the laundry bag,' added Duffy.

'What? Annie gone!' shrieked Miss Hannigan. Blowing her whistle, she ran out the orphanage door and down the street screaming, 'Bundles, come back here! Police! Police!' But Bundles and his truck were already blocks away, and Annie was gone. As they watched Miss Hannigan running crazily down the street, totally out of control, the orphans shouted with delight. 'Hooray, no more rotten smelly life for Annie!' cried Kate. And, even though they knew that they'd be punished for helping Annie to get away, they all whooped and danced with glee. All, that is, but Molly, who stood alone by the front door, her nose pressed against the cold windowpane, tears streaming down her cheeks. Her Annie was gone.

In the back of the truck, Annie had huddled inside the laundry bag without moving for about five minutes, waiting until the truck was far enough away from the orphanage for her to make her break. Now she wriggled out of the smothering bag and stood up in the dark back of the truck as it rumbled along a bumpy street. After a time, the truck came to a jerking halt, stopping for a red light, and Annie opened the back door a crack and peered out. The truck was stopped at the corner of Third Avenue and East 14th Street. Quickly, Annie hopped out, slammed the door behind her, and ran off along East 14th Street, in a moment disappearing into the crowds thronging the sidewalks that led to Union Square. Annie was free. Free – but alone, with no money and no place to live, in the middle of New York City on a chill January morning. Still, thought Annie, pulling her sweater tightly around her as the cold wind snapped down East 14th Street, she'd at least began her search for her lost father and mother.

Living in the orphanage, Annie had dimly realized that New York – and all of America – was in the midst of something called the Depression. But Annie didn't know that the Depression was the worst economic slump in the history of the country. In 1933, when the population of the United States was something less than one hundred and fifty million, more than fifteen million Americans were out of work. Millions of people were broke, homeless, and all but starving. And the Depression had hit New York harder than just about anywhere else. In New York, one person out of every three was out of work, and even those who had jobs were earning barely enough to scrape by on. In the Wall Street crash of 1929, which had started the Depression, tens of thousands of America's wealthiest industrialists and bankers and stockbrokers had been financially wiped out practically overnight. And now, in the bitterly cold winter of 1933, as the Depression reached its low point, men who'd once been presidents of banks were working as shoe-store clerks or were selling apples on New York street corners. In November of 1932, the voters of America had elected a new president, Franklin D. Roosevelt, who had promised to do something about ending the Depression. But in January of 1933, Roosevelt hadn't yet taken office, and President Hoover, who seemed to be able to do nothing about the Depression,was still in the White House. The bottom had dropped out of American life. Everything looked hopeless. So, that January day, shivering and alone on East 14th Street, Annie found herself, in every sense, out in the cold in the coldest of all possible worlds.

For hours, Annie wandered aimlessly along the chill New York sidewalks, not knowing where to begin to look for her father and mother. From time to time, she stopped a passerby, tugged on his sleeve, and, looking up, asked, 'Say, mister, did anyone you know leave a kid called Annie at an orphanage eleven years ago?' But everyone she asked either looked at her as though she were crazy and turned away or else growled, 'Nah, kid,' pushed her aside, and hurried off into the crowd. In the late afternoon, as the sun began to go down over the frozen Hudson River, the wind rose and the temperature dropped even lower, to fifteen degrees. With only her sweater to protect her from the cold, Annie's teeth were chattering loudly, and she stopped for a time to join a group of street-corner apple sellers who were huddled around a small wood fire they'd made in an ash can. She pushed her way close to the ash can and, rubbing her hands together, warmed herself at the flickering fire. Once she got warm, Annie realized that she hadn't had anything to eat all day and that she was ravenously hungry. 'Say, mister,' she said to one of the apple sellers, 'could you donate a free apple for the orphans' picnic?'

'Sure, kid, why not, nobody's buying any of them anyway,' said the apple seller.

'Gee, thanks, mister,' said Annie as he handed her a large red apple.

'Say, kid, when is the orphans' picnic?' asked the apple seller.

'As soon as I take a bite,' said Annie with a cheery grin, and she sank her teeth into the cold but juicy apple.

'Kids,' muttered the apple seller with a shake of his head. 'You can't trust nobody nowadays.'

Night came down on the wintry city, and, to try to keep warm, Annie trudged onward, block after block, heading north this time. At Seventh Avenue and West 33rd Street, she came upon a huge, pillared structure that looked like a museum but turned out to be a train station – Pennsylvania Station. Following the crowds that flowed into the station, Annie went and sat for a while in the deliciously warm waiting room. Looking around at the bedraggled people huddled on the waiting-room benches around her, Annie realized that most of them, like her, were homeless vagabonds.

Maybe I'll spend the night here, Annie thought, but then a big, beefy Irish policeman came into the waiting room and made everyone clear out unless he could show that he had a railroad ticket. Thus Annie found herself out again in the cold New York night, roaming the sidewalks that now began to grow more and more deserted. From time to time, she passed by a hot-dog stand, and the smell of frankfurters cooking on the grill made her realize that she was starving. An apple a day might keep the doctor away, thought Annie, but it sure isn't enough to keep alive on. Still, as hungry as she was, Annie kept saying over and over to herself, 'I'm glad I'm not back in the orphanage, I am, I am.'

Finally, around ten o'clock, weary from having walked about the city since eight o'clock that morning, Annie stepped out of the wind into a doorway, huddled in a corner, and pulled her sweater about her. The wind rose, and the temperature dropped. Lights were going out all over the city, and Annie thought now about the kids at the orphanage and everyone else in New York – they were safe indoors and getting into warm beds. Annie had once read in a book at school that anybody who fell asleep outdoors when the temperature was close to zero would freeze to death. And the temperature now was surely just about zero. 'I mustn't fall asleep, I mustn't,' mumbled Annie, but soon, despite her hunger and the bitter cold, she fell into a deep sleep. Annie dreamed that she was in a warm kitchen, at a table with her father and mother, and her mother was serving her a cup of hot cocoa and a huge stack of flapjacks soaked in maple syrup. Asleep in the doorway, the eleven-year-old girl had no way of knowing that she was indeed in danger of freezing to death.

FIVE

'Hey, kid, wake up, wake up!' In her dream, Annie's mother had suddenly turned into Miss Hannigan, who began shaking her by the shoulders. Now Annie opened her eyes to find herself looking up into the overly made-up face of a plump, bleached-blonde of about forty. The woman was roughly shaking her. It was close to eleven o'clock, and Annie had been asleep in the doorway for nearly an hour.

'Geez, kid, you could freeze to death out here, what the hell ya doin' sleepin' there?' said the woman.

'I . . . I didn't have any place to stay, I don't have any home,' said Annie, getting groggily to her feet.

'Oh, yeah, then you'd better come along with me to my place,' said the woman, who was bundled up in a cheap but warm grey fur coat. The woman, who said that her name was Gert Bixby, took Annie by the hand and hustled her along the freezing streets, westward towards the Hudson River. Gert Bixby had been out late at a movie and had been hurrying home when she'd chanced to spy Annie huddled in the doorway; although not normally the most warmhearted of women, she had taken pity of the sleeping child. 'Come on, come on, hurry up, before we both freeze to death,' said Gert.

Ahead of them, at the corner of Twelfth Avenue and West 45th Street, by the waterfront, Annie saw a

46

blinking red neon sign that read BIXBY'S BEANERY, EATS. 'This here is the place,' said Gert as they reached the Beanery and stepped out of the cold into the steamy warmth of the waterfront restaurant. Brightly lighted and smelling rankly of greasy food, Bixby's Beanery consisted of a scarred wooden counter with a dozen or so stools, and a half dozen red leatherette booths. The place was all but empty. A couple of longshoremen were drinking coffee in one of the booths, and a fat, bald, florid-faced man who was reading the New York *Daily Mirror* behind the counter turned out to be Gert's husband, Fred Bixby. 'Who the hell's that ya got with ya?' asked Fred with a scowl, wiping his hands on his stained white apron as he nodded towards Annie. 'Some kid I found sleepin' out in the cold – she ain't got no place to stay,' said Gert, wriggling out of her fur coat and turning to Annie. 'So, what's your name, kid?' Gert asked.

'Annie,' said Annie, still shivering from the cold although her cheeks and fingers burned painfully from the sudden warmth of the Beanery.

'Ya hungry, Annie?' Gert asked.

'Well . . .' said Annie.

'Sit down at the counter and Fred'll serve ya up a plate of beans, won't ya, Fred?' said Gert.

'What are we runnin' here, a free kitchen for bums?' grumbled Fred. 'I'm not . . .'

'Shut up your yap, Fred, and give the kid some beans,' said Gert.

'Ahhh,' said Fred, but he ladled out a steaming bowl of brown-crusted baked beans and set it on the counter in front of Annie, who quickly gobbled down every last bit. The beans were mushy and slightly rancid, but they tasted better to Annie than anything she'd ever eaten. Bixby's Beanery wasn't a very pleasant place, thought Annie, and Gert and Fred Bixby didn't seem all that pleasant, either, but at least, she said to herself, I'm in out of the cold and I've had something to eat.

Fred and Gert, Annie soon learned, ran the Beanery together, sharing the work fifty-fifty and living at the back in a small, cluttered two-room apartment. Business was bad for the Bixbys – there were many in the Depression who couldn't even afford a dime to buy a doughnut and a cup of coffee. But Fred and Gert were able to squeeze out a living from the Beanery as long as they did all the work themselves. So Fred served as counterman, short-order cook, and dishwasher while Gert was the Beanery's cashier and only waitress. But even though they were getting by, they were scarcely happy with their lot. Fred's favourite pastimes were drinking, betting on horses, and sleeping, but he didn't get much of a chance to indulge himself, for the Beanery opened at seven o'clock each morning and didn't close until midnight. Gert loved going to the movies, but Fred gave her time off only once every couple of weeks. Luckily for Annie, tonight had been Gert's night out – she'd been on her way home from seeing Clark Gable in *Manhandled* when she'd spied Annie in the doorway.

Now, seeing that Annie was still hungry, Gert went behind the counter and, ignoring Fred's angry glances, served her up a piece of apple pie and a cup of hot chocolate. 'Gee, thanks, Mrs Bixby,' said Annie, digging eagerly into the pie. As Annie ate, Gert drew

48

Fred into the apartment at the back, and Annie could hear fragments of a heated conversation. A couple of minutes later, when Fred came back out front with Gert, he smiled at Annie for the first time since she'd come into the Beanery – a crooked, gap-toothed smile.

'So, kid, you don't have no place to stay, how'd you like to stay here with us?' asked Fred with oily geniality, leaning over to pat Annie on the head.

'Here?' said Annie. She couldn't understand Mr Bixby's sudden change of attitude towards her. And, she noticed, it certainly wasn't reflected in his cold, scheming eyes.

'Yeah – here,' said Fred. 'We ain't got no more room in our apartment, but there's a furnace down in the cellar, real warm, and there's a cot down there. We give ya a couple of blankets and you'll be snug as a bug in a rug.'

'Gee, I don't know, sir,' said Annie, 'I . . .'

'Look, Annie, whatta ya gonna do, sleep outside in that cold?' said Gert. 'We give ya a place to bunk, free eats, and maybe ya do a little work around the joint for us.'

'Well . . . all right,' said Annie, and soon she found herself being tucked by Gert into the cot down in the cellar furnace room. The tiny windowless room was filthy and reeked of coal fumes, but it was nonetheless warm and cozy, and within a few minutes, after Gert had switched out the lights and gone back upstairs, Annie had fallen deeply asleep.

While Annie had been eating the apple pie at the counter, Gert had been trying to persuade Fred back in the apartment that finding the lost child could be a

49

stroke of good luck for them. 'Can't ya see she's as strong as a little ox,' Gert argued. 'We keep her here, it costs us nothin' but a few pennies a day in extra food, and we get ourselves a free waitress, a free dishwasher, a free janitor to clean up the joint.'

'Hmm, yeah, I didn't think of that,' Fred said. 'But, hey, the kid must belong somewheres – we don't wanna get into no trouble with the cops.'

'Ahh, she's a runaway – probably got a ma and pa that beat her,' Gert said. 'And nobody's ever gonna find her here. Anybody asks any questions, we just say she's our niece come to live with us from Cleveland.'

'Yeah,' Fred said, warming to the idea. 'You know, Gert, sometimes you're not as dumb as you look.' And it was then that Fred had come out to the counter and suddenly been so friendly to Annie.

A light clicked on in the furnace room. Somebody was once again roughly shaking Annie awake. It was Fred Bixby. 'Come on, kiddo, you don't get to sleep to noon around here, it's six-thirty, rise and shine,' Fred growled. 'Ya gonna stay here, ya gotta work for your keep.'

'Yes, sir,' said Annie, getting dazedly up from her cot – for a moment, she hadn't remembered where she was. A while later, upstairs, Annie was togged out in a bottle-green waitress's uniform that hung almost to her ankles. 'What do you want to do first?' Gert asked her. 'I don't know,' said Annie. 'Well, why don't ya start by washin' all the windows in the place,' said Gert. 'Yes, ma'am,' replied Annie. Later, after she'd finished the windows, Fred taught her how to make coffee in the huge urn behind the counter and how to work the cash register. All day, from seven o'clock in the morning until midnight, when the doors were finally locked and the flashing neon sign turned off, Annie toiled in the Beanery – mopping the floors, scrubbing pots and pans, cleaning the greasy griddle, serving at the counter, and scurrying about to wait on the customers in the booths. By the end of the day, Annie was so tired that she dropped off to sleep with one of her shoes still on as she fell back onto her cot by the furnace. Only to be awakened to start all over again at six-thirty the following morning.

As the cold days of January passed, Annie left the Beanery to breathe fresh air only when toting pails of garbage outside to the back alley. In the Beanery, she spent a good deal of her time being tutored by Fred in the art of short-order cooking. She learned how to cook home-fried potatoes, omelettes, and Mulligan stew, to grill hot dogs and hamburgers, to make Boston baked beans, and to mix up batches of chicken, tuna-fish, and egg salads. Within a few weeks, in fact, Annie was a far better short-order cook than Fred had ever been, and he stepped aside to let her take over the cooking. And, of course, he was delighted to let her take the job. For now, with Annie at the stove behind the counter, Fred was free to spend a large portion of his days getting soddenly drunk in a nearby speakeasy called McGuire's.

Although she had to work even harder when he wasn't around to help, Annie was far happier in the Beanery when Fred Bixby was down the street at McGuire's. For he frightened her terribly. 'Look, kid, I know you're a runaway from somewheres,' Fred had said to her one day shortly after she'd come to the Beanery, 'but you try to run away from here and I'll catch you, I promise, and give you such a beatin' with this belt of mine that you won't forget it for the rest of your days.' So, although she often thought of running away from the Beanery, she was afraid that if she did Fred would catch her and beat her even worse than Miss Hannigan ever had. Besides, her day out in New York in the winter had made her realize that until spring came along it was wiser to be warm indoors and eating regularly than to be freezing outdoors and starving. No matter how hard she had to work.

Annie was happier in the Beanery, too, on those frequent evenings when Gert Bixby was off at the movies. For since Annie was on hand to do all of the waiting on customers, Gert now went to the movies three or four evenings a week. During the day, however, Gert was always around. She sat from morning until night perched on a stool by the cash register, where, chomping vigorously on enormous wads of chewing gum, she listened to the radio while reading endless movie magazines. Gert rarely looked up from her magazines other than to ring up a bill or to bark orders at Annie. 'For God's sake, Annie, are you blind?' she'd complain. 'There's customers in booth three that ain't been waited on!' (The customers would be just taking off their coats.) Or, 'Don't stand around all day, Annie, clean off the counter for that man.' And even when there were no customers in the Beanery and Annie had sat down briefly to take a breather, Gert kept at her. 'Come on, Annie, get off your lazy backside – those sugar bowls want fillin'.' So Gert's evenings at the movies amounted almost to time off for Annie, especially when Fred also went out to McGuire's.

Indeed, Annie's only happy times at the Beanery were when she was left alone by the Bixbys to run the place by herself. The Beanery's customers were rough and boisterous but friendly – longshoremen who worked on the West Side docks, sailors off ships that put in at the docks, and neighbourhood regulars, like Vinnie and Al, who worked at a nearby Texaco station. Word had quickly gotten around the West Side that someone was doing some mighty good cooking in Bixby's Beanery, and everyone was soon flocking to the restaurant for one of Annie's omelettes or a bowl of her Mulligan stew. The luncheon trade all but doubled and the dinner business picked up considerably, too, much to the delight of the Bixbys. 'That kid is a goddamn jewel and we ain't lettin' her get away from us,' said Fred to Gert. The customers liked Annie, too, for she always greeted them with a smile and a cheery, 'How are you today, sir?' 'You know somethin', Annie,' joked Vinnie, 'when you grow up, I'm gonna marry you – for your cookin' alone.' 'Yeah,' said Al. 'Rockefeller can have his barrels of money – we got Annie.' The evening hours had a certain sweetness for Annie when Fred and Gert were gone and just the regular customers were on hand – people like Vinnie and Al were the first grown-ups who had ever been nice to her. Still, she longed to get away from the drudgery of the Beanery, and sometimes, when lying on her cot before falling asleep at night, she wondered if she'd have been better off if she'd never run away from Miss Hannigan and the orphanage.

Even though her school days hadn't been happy days, she missed P.S. 62 and the chance to read and to learn. She was worried about missing the entire second half of sixth grade. But I'll be back in school next fall, Annie promised herself, somehow or other, come what may. Working in the Beanery wasn't getting her any closer to finding her father and mother, either, Annie sadly reflected, and that had been the reason, after all, that she'd run away from the orphanage in the first place. Of course, the Bixbys had allowed her to post a handwritten sign by the cash register that said, 'Anybody who knows of anybody who left a baby named Annie at a New York City orphanage eleven years ago please contact Annie behind the counter. Annie.' But no one had ever contacted her. Also, whenever a customer came into the Beanery who looked even a little bit as though he might be her father, she would go up to him and say, 'Pardon me, mister, but did you happen to leave a baby named Annie at an orphanage a few years ago?' But the answer was always no.

The days at the Beanery passed by in a blur for Annie, and later there was only one day that stood out separately in her memory of that time, March 20th, 1933, when she, the Bixbys, and several customers had grouped around Gert's radio by the cash register to listen to Franklin D. Roosevelt being sworn in in Washington as the new President of the United States. Annie would always remember Roosevelt's inaugural speech, when he promised America that he would bring an end to the Depression and spoke the ringing words,

54

'The only thing we have to fear is fear itself!' Fear itself, thought Annie. I guess he's never met Miss Hannigan. Or Fred Bixby.

Suddenly, spring came to New York City, and the leaves on a forlorn, stunted ginkgo tree outside the Beanery miraculously began to come into bud. The days grew warm and the coal furnace in the cellar of the Beanery, which Annie had had to stoke several times a day, was turned off. And now she slept without blankets in her dark little cellar room. Shortly before noon, on a grey, drizzly day in early May, Gert ordered her to carry a can of garbage out to the back alley behind the Beanery. As Annie came out the door, she spied a pair of teen-aged toughs throwing paving stones at a small boy who was cowering behind a row of garbage cans at the far end of the alley. Putting down the garbage can she was toting, Annie called out to them, 'Hey, you two bullies, stop throwin' them stones at the poor kid!'

'What kid, you dumb little twerp?' said the bigger of the two toughs, a burly redhead of about fourteen. 'It ain't no kid, it's a dog.'

'A dog, that's even worse,' said Annie, advancing towards the two boys. 'I said, stop throwin' them stones!'

'Oh, yeah, you and who else is gonna make us?' said the other boy, who was dark-haired, sallow-faced, and perhaps three inches taller than Annie. He flung another stone at the dog.

'Me and nobody else,' said Annie, walking up to the dark-haired boy, whom the other boy called Augie, and giving him a shove in the chest.

'Oh, so you wanna fight, huh?' said Augie.

'Yeah, I wanna fight.' Annie stood still.

Augie swung a roundhouse punch that Annie ducked in one quick movement. Coming up, she hit Augie in the face with a hard overhand right that sent him sprawling to the ground. A bit of blood trickled from his nose.

'You little bully, look what ya done – my nose is bleedin',' whined Augie as Annie stood above him with clenched fists.

'Yeah, and you'll get worse than a bloody nose if you don't leave that poor dog alone and get outta here – scram!' ordered Annie.

'Okay, I'm goin',' said Augie, getting warily to his feet and shouting to the bigger, redheaded boy, who'd crept behind Annie, 'Get her, Eddie! Beat her brains out!'

'I got her!' snarled Eddie, but Annie whirled around just in time to block a punch and to land a left uppercut to the jaw that knocked Eddie off his feet. Upon seeing that Eddie, too, was getting the worst of it from Annie, Augie ran off, whimpering, 'I'm gettin' outta here.'

Eddie got groggily to his feet, but Annie quickly knocked him down again with a whirlwind of right and left hooks. 'Okay,' she said, standing over him, 'you had enough?'

'Yeah, okay, I had enough,' Eddie muttered, and he quickly scrambled up and ran off, calling back over his shoulder, 'But I woulda beat ya if you'da fought fair, you sissy little girl.'

'Get goin'!' Annie shouted after him. 'But anytime you want more, come on back!' Annie rubbed her knuckles, heaved a sigh, and turned to the dog, who was still cowering behind the garbage cans. Annie got down

56

on her knees, patted the ground in front of her, and called gently to the frightened dog. 'Here, boy, come on, boy, there's nothing to be afraid of now.' For a moment, the dog didn't move, but then, reassured by the kindness in Annie's voice, he crept out from behind the garbage can and came tentatively up to her. He was a large shaggy coffee-coloured mongrel with huge sad and soulful eyes. 'Ah, poor boy, did they hurt you?' Annie murmured softly, stroking the dog. Annie noticed that he had a short piece of rope strung around his neck that looked as though it had been gnawed through by the dog. 'I'll bet you're a runaway, like me, from folks that treated you bad,' said Annie to the dog as he nuzzled against her. 'Well, nobody's gonna hurt you no more, ever, because you're gonna be *my* dog.'

'Annie, Annie, where the hell are you?' screamed Gert, coming angrily out the back door into the alley. 'How long does it take to put out one garbage can?'

'Look, Mrs Bixby, a stray dog – I found him out here in the alley,' said Annie. 'Can I keep him?'

Gert looked down in disgust at Annie and the dog. 'Can you keep him?' said Gert sarcastically. 'Of course you can keep him. And for his food, three times a day, maybe he'd like a nice juicy sirloin steak? And a place to sleep? Why, he can have my bed.'

'Please, Mrs Bixby, please,' begged Annie. 'He can have half of my food and he can sleep down in the furnace room with me. So, he wouldn't cost you nothin' and he wouldn't be no bother, I promise.'

'Yeah, that's all we need around the Beanery, a big dumb mutt like that,' Gert said scornfully. 'I know what I'm doin'. I'm goin' inside right now and callin' the dog pound. Have 'em come and take this mangy mongrel away. They'll take care of him. Good care. Whatta ya call it? Oh, yeah. Put him to sleep.'

'Oh, please, Mrs Bixby, you wouldn't do that, please, please,' pleaded Annie.

'I wouldn't, huh – just you wait and see,' Gert replied. 'Now, you leave that damn dog here and get back inside to work – there's customers to be waited on.'

'Yes, Mrs Bixby, I'll be there in just a minute,' said Annie as Gert went stomping back into the Beanery. But Annie wasn't going to abandon the dog. 'Don't worry, boy, I'm not gonna let them get you,' said Annie, and at once she made up her mind. She and the dog were going to run away. Far away. Where neither the men from the dog pound nor Fred Bixby would ever find them. And right now. Quickly, telling the dog that she'd be right back, Annie tied him to the handle of a garbage can and raced downstairs to the furnace room, where she got hurriedly out of her waitress uniform and into the dress and sweater she'd been wearing when she'd arrived at the Beanery in January. Once again, she packed her few belongings in her wicker basket, and in less than a minute she was back in the alley. She untied the dog and the two of them were on their way. 'Come on, boy, we gotta hurry, run!' called Annie, and the little girl and the dog fled from the alley and ran eastward along West 45th Street, away from the river and towards midtown Manhattan. As they ran, Annie felt herself filled suddenly with joy. For it dawned on her that she'd said good-bye forever to Fred, Gert, and Bixby's Beanery. She was homeless again, of course, adrift in the vast city without a penny. But the drizzly May morning was at least warm, and this time she wasn't running away alone. She had a dog. A dog of her own!

SIX

Annie and the dog had gone only three blocks when they were stopped by a harsh voice calling out, 'Hey, you, little girl, come here!' Oh, no, thought Annie, her heart sinking, the Bixbys have already got the police after me. Turning, she saw that the man who'd shouted at her was indeed a policeman, tall and burly and menacingly swinging his nightstick. 'Yes, officer?' said Annie sweetly, trying to act very innocent as she dropped the dog's rope and strolled up to him.

'That dog over there,' said the policeman, 'ain't I seen him runnin' around the neighbourhood? Ain't he a stray?'

Annie gulped. 'A stray?' she managed to get out. 'Oh, no, officer. He's . . . he's my dog.'

'Your dog, huh?' said the policeman sceptically. 'So, what's his name?'

'His name?' said Annie, looking first at the policeman and then over at the dog, stalling for time, trying to think as fast as she could. 'His name is . . . Sandy. Right, that's it, Sandy. I call him Sandy, you see, because of his nice sandy colour.'

'Sandy colour, huh?' repeated the policeman, still not believing her. 'Okay, let's see him answer to his name.'

'Answer?' said Annie, gulping again. 'You mean . . . when I call him?'

'Right,' said the policeman. 'When you call him. By his name. Sandy.'

'Well, you see, officer,' said Annie, 'I just got him and sometimes he doesn't answer when . . .'

'Call him!' snapped the policeman.

'Okay,' said Annie with a sigh, turning to the dog, and patting her knees. 'Here, Sandy. Here, boy. Come on, Sandy.'

For what seemed to Annie like forever, the dog stood motionless, staring uncertainly at her with his huge woebegone eyes. But then his eyes suddenly brightened, and he trotted over to Annie and jumped up to put his paws on her shoulders.

'Good Sandy,' said Annie, smiling from ear to ear. 'Good old Sandy!'

'Hmm,' said the policeman. 'Well, maybe he is your dog. But next time you take him out I wanna see him on a leash and with a licence. Or else he goes to the dog pound. And that'll be the end of him. You understand?'

'Yes, sir, I understand,' said Annie. 'On a leash and with a licence.'

'Now, get along home with you, you and your dog,' said the policeman, turning and walking off down the sidewalk.

'Yes, officer,' said Annie. As soon as the policeman was out of sight around a corner, Annie and the dog took off running again, hurrying to get as far as they could from Bixby's Beanery. Sandy, thought Annie as they ran, that's the perfect name for my beautiful new dog. And from that moment on he was Sandy, forever.

At last, out of breath from having run without stopping for nearly half an hour, Annie pulled Sandy

61

into an alley and they sat down to rest. 'Good Sandy,' said Annie, gently patting the dog. Sandy, she saw, still looked sad and frightened. 'Don't worry, Sandy, I'll take care of you, good care,' said Annie. 'And everything's gonna be fine. For the both of us. If not today, well . . .' Annie looked up at the leaden sky. 'The sun'll come out tomorrow,' said Annie quietly. 'You can bet your bottom dollar that tomorrow there'll be sun.' Sandy's large brown eyes seemed suddenly to become more trusting, and he licked her face with his big red tongue. She smiled. He likes me, Annie happily realized, as much as I like him. It began to rain harder. Annie shook her head, gazed at the sky, and said wryly to herself, 'I love you tomorrow, 'cause you're always a day away.'

'Come on, Sandy,' urged Annie, 'we gotta find ourselves someplace to stay tonight, in out of this darn rain, and we gotta find some way to get ourselves somethin' to eat.' Staying close to the buildings so as not to get drenched in the rain, the small girl and her out-sized dog hurried eastward along the wet New York sidewalks. They looked up in awe as they passed through a part of the city that, Annie later found out, was called Times Square – it was a dazzle of movie theatres and enormous, brightly coloured neon signs that flashed on and off in the dark, rainy afternoon. No one seemed even to notice Annie and Sandy in the crowds of people hurrying in all directions. Before long, they came upon a large grey granite building – it was Grand Central Station. 'Good, we can get in out of the rain here,' Annie told Sandy, and she led him through a doorway and down a flight of marble stairs to the main concourse of the station, the biggest room that Annie had ever seen. 'Wow, Sandy, look at this place, how'd you like to live here?' said Annie, her eyes bright with wonder at the huge hall and its ceiling of painted stars. For a time, happy to be in out of the rain, Annie and Sandy wandered about the station, jostled by the crowds hustling to and from trains. 'Someday, I'll find my father and mother and they'll take us on a train trip, maybe to the seashore or the mountains,' Annie promised Sandy.

As the rainy afternoon passed into evening, Annie felt herself growing hungrier and hungrier. And she suspected that Sandy was hungry, too. 'We gotta find ourselves some way to make some money, so's we can buy somethin' to eat,' explained Annie to Sandy, and then she spied an apple seller standing by the Lexington Avenue entrance with a tray of apples strung about his neck. 'Apples, apples, two for ten get your nice rosy-red apples,' the man cried over and over again, but no one stopped to buy apples from him. He was a haggard, unshaven man in a threadbare brown suit that must have seen better days before the Depression, but he had friendly eyes, and Annie decided to take a chance on speaking to him. 'Excuse me, mister,' she said, 'but where do you get the apples to sell?'

'Thinking of going into business, little lady?' asked the man cheerfully.

'Well, I don't know. Maybe.'

'I get them at a wholesale fruit market over by the East River,' the man told her. 'They sell for a penny apiece, a hundred for a dollar, and I sell them for a nickel apiece, thus making a handsome profit of four cents per apple. That, my little lady, is what we Americans call capitalism. Buy low and sell high. A few years ago, I was doing it with stocks and bonds, and now I'm in the retail-apple game. But I can't complain. You sell yourself a thousand apples a day and you make yourself forty dollars.

'Wow!' Annie exclaimed. 'How many have you sold today?'

'Three,' said the man with a rueful laugh, 'for a net profit of twelve cents. But things are looking up. Yesterday I only sold two.'

'Oh,' said Annie. She tried to sound enthusiastic.

'Tell me, little lady,' asked the apple seller, 'are you hungry?'

'Well, I . . .'

'Of course you are. Everybody is.' And he handed her a pair of apples. 'Here you go, my dear,' he said graciously, 'one for you and one for your large dog, compliments of the management.'

'Gee, thanks, mister!' Annie quickly fed one of the apples to Sandy, who wolfed it down in three bites, and gobbled up the other herself.

A little bit of her hunger gone, Annie looked outside – she saw that the rain had stopped. But the evening had grown sharply cooler; it was going to be a cold night. 'We gotta find ourselves someplace to stay tonight,' Annie told Sandy. And then she had an idea. She lingered with Sandy near Lexington Avenue entrance for the next two hours, watching the apple seller trying unsuccessfully to sell his apples to commuters hurrying to catch trains that would take them to their homes in the suburbs. By seven-thirty, however, few people were coming into the station, and now, Annie saw, the apple seller gave up and started off into the cool May night. 'Come on, Sandy, we're gonna follow him,' said Annie.

As Annie and Sandy trailed in the shadows, the apple seller trudged up Lexington Avenue to East 59th Street and then headed eastward towards the East River. There he disappeared over the edge of an embankment next to the 59th Street bridge, seemingly headed straight into the river. Annie and Sandy ran to the embankment and looked down. Below them, under the bridge at the river's edge, they saw a makeshift little camp – there were maybe a dozen shanties. In the middle of the camp, shadowy figures were huddled around fires that blazed up fitfully from ash cans. At the largest of the fires, a woman appeared to be cooking something in a huge cauldron that hung on a spit. Their friend, the apple seller, Annie saw, was warming himself by one of the fires. 'Gee, Sandy, I wonder what this place is?' Annie whispered.

In New York, in the Depression, thousands of homeless people, many of whom had once lived in elegant Park Avenue and Riverside Drive apartments banded together to live in shanty-towns that – mockingly named after President Hoover, on whom many blamed the Depression – were known as Hoovervilles. The floorless shanties were slapped together from scrap wood, cardboard, and pieces of iron, with sheets of corrugated tin for roofs. Dirty, ugly, without heat or ventilation, the shanties had no virtues other than that they provided a roof over one's head. The rich of New York, who still numbered in the thousands in 1933, looked upon the Hoovervilles as an eyesore and a

65

disgrace to the city, and they were constantly after the Mayor to have them torn down. But, argued the Mayor, it was better to have the homeless living in Hoovervilles than sleeping in doorways, like Bowery bums, and so the Hoovervilles were tolerated – or ignored – by the city authorities, including the police. It was such a Hooverville that Annie and Sandy had come upon.

'Let's go, Sandy, I don't know what this place is but at least they've got fires to keep warm by,' said Annie, leading her dog down the steep embankment towards the Hooverville below. 'And, hey, maybe we can find us somethin' to eat. Come on!' The men and women gathered in the shadows around the flickering fires were thin, shabbily dressed, and sad-looking, but they didn't appear to be at all mean or unfriendly. They looked like the dazed survivors of some terrible catastrophe, which, of course, they were. 'Pardon me, folks,' said Annie, nervously clearing her throat as she neared the group around one of the fires, 'but did anybody here leave a redheaded kid named Annie at an orphanage eleven years ago?' A few of the people huddled around the fire and said 'No' or 'Uh-uh, kid,' but most of them simply ignored her question. Figuring that no one would mind, Annie stepped up close to the fire and held out her hands over the flames.

The woman who'd been cooking now banged an iron spoon against the side of the cauldron and hoarsely called out, 'Ladies and gents, put on a smile, dinner is served! The stew is on!' At once, everyone scurried about, got spoons and tin cans, and lined up to be served. The people in the Hooverville lived communally, each chipping in a few pennies a day to the cook,

66

Sophie, who bought vegetables, potatoes, and cheap cuts of meat to make a hot stew every night. Her stew wasn't very good, but at least it was hot food on a cold night. As she was ladling out the stew, Sophie glanced at Annie and Sandy, who were standing off in the shadows. 'Hey, kid, you hungry?' asked Sophie.

'Naw,' said Annie. She was too proud to admit that she was starving. 'But my dog is.'

'Come on then, kid,' said Sophie, beckoning to Annie and handing her a spoon and an empty Campbell's soup can, 'and bring your dog, too.'

'Gee, thanks, lady,' said Annie as Sophie filled up her soup can with a steaming ladleful of stew.

'Call me Sophie, everybody else does,' said Sophie, flashing a toothless smile. She was a short, plump woman with a round and friendly face. She wore the shabbiest getup that Annie had ever seen on anyone – a dress of faded tan and yellow patches that looked to be made out of leftover pieces of canvas, and fraying strips of burlap around her feet in place of shoes. But Sophie certainly seemed to be cheerful.

'I'm Annie, and this is Sandy.' Annie made a polite little bow.

'Pleased to meet ya, Annie,' said Sophie. 'Eat your fill, you and your Sandy. And there's plenty more where that came from.'

In the orange light from the ash-can fires, everyone sat in a circle on the ground and ate. With great appetite, Annie took a huge spoonful of the stew. 'Yecccchh,' she said to herself. She'd never tasted anything so terrible in her life, and that included Miss Hannigan's mush. Still, it was food. She ate half of the canful and passed the rest along to Sandy. He clearly didn't like it very much, either. But he ate it. If nothing else, Sophie's stew was filling, and people ate anything they could get in those dark Depression days, to survive.

The apple seller whom Annie and Sandy had followed to the Hooverville from Grand Central Station came up to the group. 'Say, kid, haven't I seen you somewhere before?' he asked introducing himself to Annie as G. Randall Whitworth, Jr., or Randy to his friends.

'Well, I . . .' said Annie.

'Of course,' said Randy, 'you're the little girl who was hanging around the station all afternoon. What'd you do, follow me here?'

'Well, yes, I guess so,' admitted Annie, a little ashamed of what she had done.

'Ahh, that's all right, kid, at the bottom of life's ladder there's always room for one more,' Randy assured her. 'So, little lady, what are you doing out alone at this time of night?'

'I'm . . . I'm looking for my mum and dad,' Annie explained. 'They're lost.'

'Lost, huh?' said Randy. 'How long have you been looking for them?'

'Eleven years,' said Annie.

'Now, that's *lost*,' Randy agreed.

'Don't worry, Annie, you'll find them,' Sophie assured her.

'You're darned right I'll find them,' said Annie with confidence.

'Well, well, there's something I haven't heard since 1928,' drawled Randy.

68

'What?' asked Sophie.

'Optimism,' explained Randy with a loud laugh.

'What have we got to be optimistic about?' asked a gloomy-faced man named Lou as he held out his tin can for more stew. 'Look at us. Look at this dump. Life's a nightmare.'

'Well, you gotta have a dream,' said Annie with a grin.

'Huh,' grunted Lou. 'Under this goddamn bridge, traffic rattlin' overhead all night.'

'To wake you up from your nightmare,' answered Annie. Everyone around the fire laughed.

'It ain't funny, kid,' said Lou sourly. 'Not when all you got in the world is empty pockets.'

'At least you got pockets,' Annie rejoined. 'Lots of folks these days don't, I'll bet.'

'Freezin' fingers,' muttered Lou.

'Lucky thing you got them empty pockets to put 'em in,' replied Annie. Once again, everyone laughed.

'All right, kid, you're so smart,' said Lou. 'You know what else we got here? Newspapers for blankets. Now, whatta you say to that?'

Everyone was silent around the fire as Annie thought for a moment. 'I got it,' Annie said, smiling. 'You can read in bed!'

'Ahh, I give up,' said Lou, getting up from the fire and walking away in disgust while the others laughed with delight at Annie's cheerful victory.

'You know something, Annie?' said Randy. 'You're okay.'

'Annie,' asked Sophie, 'you got yourself a place to stay for the night?'

'Well, uh, not exactly,' Annie replied. 'You see, I kind of ran away from . . .'

Randy stopped her. 'Uh-uh, Annie, don't tell us,' he said. 'Down here at the bottom of life's pickle barrel, we don't ask anybody questions about why they're here. We don't talk about our pasts and we don't talk about our futures. We just try to help each other to get through the present – one day at a time, as they say up at Sing Sing. And our present, I might add, happens to stink. Some business I'm in. Seven million people in New York, and today I managed to sell seven apples. In the rain, yet.'

'The sun'll come out tomorrow,' said Annie. 'You can bet your bottom dollar that tomorrow there'll be sun.'

'I would, kid, if I hadn't already lost my bottom dollar,' Randy laughed.

'Look, Annie, if you need a place to stay you can bunk in with me,' Sophie offered. 'I got a little tin palace over there all to myself and there's plenty of room for the both of us.'

'For Sandy, too?' Annie asked.

'For Sandy, too, of course,' said Sophie good-naturedly, and later, when the fires had died down and everyone had begun to get ready for the night, Sophie lighted a candle and led Annie and Sandy into he shanty. The roof was so low that Sophie had to bend down when she was inside, although Annie could stand up fine. The shanty smelled of mildew and candle wax, but it was at least warm and dry. Sophie spread three layers of newspapers on the hard dirt floor of the shanty to make a bed for Annie and Sandy, and the child and the dog lay down on the bed, nestled together. Then

Sophie covered them over with three more layers of newspapers. The newspapers made a surprisingly comfortable and cozy – if crackly – bed, Annie discovered, and, putting her arms around Sandy's neck, she soon fell asleep.

'Good night, sleep tight, and don't let the bed bugs bite,' whispered Sophie, blowing out the candle and settling heavily down on a similar bed of newspapers at the other side of the shanty. In the middle of the night, the rain began to fall again, pelting the corrugated tin roof of the shanty with a sound that was almost as loud as gunfire. Sophie woke up abruptly. But Annie and Sandy was so tired that they slept right through the storm. Sophie lighted a candle in the dark and looked over at the sleeping child and her dog. 'What a sweet little girl,' said Sophie softly. It was too bad that Annie couldn't have heard Sophie, for that was almost the first time in her life that anyone had ever said anything nice about her.

SEVEN

The next morning, the rain had stopped but the sun hadn't come out – it was a bleak, grey day. In the shanty, Annie was awakened by Randy calling to her, 'Come on, little lady, rise and shine. You and I are going into business together!' Randy explained a few minutes later that he'd decided to give her some of his extra apples to sell and that they'd split the profits fifty-fifty. 'I'm branching out – taking on hired help,' explained Randy grandly, smiling as the Hoovervillites sat around on the ground outside their shanties eating oatmeal that Sophie had cooked up for breakfast. Sophie's oatmeal, Annie decided, was slightly more tasty than Miss Hannigan's mush. But not much more. After breakfast, fitted out with a cardboard tray of apples strung about her neck on a piece of twine, Annie set out with Sandy and Randy for Grand Central Station. There Randy positioned her by the Lexington Avenue entrance, and he went around to the Vanderbilt Avenue entrance. 'A little tyke like you, you're bound to sell plenty of apples,' said Randy, 'so long as you look sad and hungry.'

'That won't be hard,' Annie exclaimed cheerfully as Randy left her to sell her wares. 'Apples, apples, five cents apiece, two for a dime!' Annie cried out to the travellers hurrying in and out of the station. 'Remember, folks, an apple a day keeps the doctor away.

72

And two apples a day keeps two doctors away!'

All day long, from eight o'clock in the morning until after seven o'clock at night, with only an occasional break to rest on one of the benches in the Grand Central waiting room, Annie sold apples. And ate apples. Annie and Sandy each had an apple for lunch and another for a late-afternoon snack. 'We're eatin' up the profits,' said Annie to Sandy, 'but we gotta keep up our strength if we're gonna make it through the day.' At seven-fifteen, when Randy rejoined them, he was delighted to learn that Annie had sold seventeen apples and taken in eighty-five cents. (He had sold only five that day.) 'Aw, it was nothin',' shrugged Annie, smiling proudly as she handed the money over to Randy.

'Nothing? It's a small fortune,' said Randy happily. 'I knew it – I knew they'd buy more apples from a nice-looking kid like you than from a no-good-looking bum like me. Annie, you and I are going to get rich!'

Randy handed Annie her share of the money – thirty-four cents. She tucked it into the pocket of her sweater – it was more money than she'd ever had before in her life. And then the three of them – Annie, Sandy, and Randy – trudged back uptown to the Hooverville, where they were just in time for a helping of Sophie's stew. To pay for her keep, Annie gave half of the money she'd earned that day – seventeen cents – to Sophie. She kept the other half. 'I'm gonna save up and buy bus tickets,' Annie earnestly told Sophie, 'and then me and Sandy, we're gonna go all over America, all over the world if we have to, lookin' for my mum and dad, until we find them. And we're gonna find them, we are!' 'Of course you are,' said Sophie, gently tousling Annie's hair.

73

After dinner in the Hooverville, as a full moon came up in the pale-blue sky above the 59th Street bridge, they all sat on the ground in the warm May night and talked yearningly about what they were going to do after the Depression was over. Lou began to play the harmonica, and soon the ragged group was singing along old songs like 'By the Light of the Silvery Moon' and 'Moonlight Bay'. Around ten o'clock, Annie said good night and led Sandy to their bed of newspapers in Sophie's shanty. Carefully covering Sandy with papers, Annie lay on the bed next to him and put her arms around his neck. 'You know, Sandy, we're doin' all right for ourselves,' she said quietly to the dog as she heard the grown-ups outside talking and singing in the warm spring night. 'We got a place to stay, food, friends, and even a job. I mean, look at us, we're already seventeen cents rich!' And, as the bright full moon shone down on the Hooverville shanty, Annie and Sandy soon fell asleep.

A new life had begun for Annie. And Sandy. In the weeks that followed, as spring gave way to summer in New York, the girl and her dog went with Randy each day to Grand Central Station and took up their stand. With spirit and determination, they sold apples until nightfall. They had their good days and their bad days, but there wasn't a day when Annie didn't end up making at least ten cents. And by the middle of August, she'd saved up $13.25.

Although the residents of the Hooverville often sang and laughed and joked, their life was a hard one. Broke, out of work, scrounging for pennies to pay for their

74

share of the food, and sleeping under newspapers in tumbledown shanties, they had little hope of ever finding a real job again or of ever getting out of the Hooverville. And life in the Hooverville wasn't easy for Annie, either, although she tried always to have a cheery smile on her face. Annie got up each morning full of hope, convinced that the day ahead would at last be the day when she'd find her father and mother. But each night she went to bed disappointed. 'Tomorrow,' Annie would say to herself with a sigh before she closed her eyes and dropped wearily off to sleep. 'Yes, tomorrow will be the day.'

As she walked back and forth with Randy between the Hooverville and Grand Central Station, Annie told him about her life in the orphanage and how she'd run away to find her father and mother. And Randy helped her letter a large cardboard sign that she propped next to her by the entrance to Grand Central Station: 'Anyone having any information about anyone who left a two-month-old infant named Annie at a New York City orphanage on the night of December 31st, 1921, please contact the young lady selling apples beside this sign. Reward $13.25.' And each week, as she saved more money, Annie raised the amount of the reward, until by early October it had risen to $23.75. But although hundreds of people stopped to read the sign every day, not one of them ever had any information about her father and mother. Still, Randy continued to keep up her hopes. 'I promise you, Annie, sooner or later everyone in America passes through Grand Central Station,' said Randy, 'so you couldn't be in a more ideal place. If you stand here long enough, you're bound to find your parents.'

The thought that everyone in America eventually passed through Grand Central Station heartened Annie. But it also made her nervous when she realized that everyone in America included Fred Bixby. For she lived in constant fear that Fred would swoop down on her while she was selling apples, drag her across town, beat her unmercifully, and force her to work once again in the Beanery. Still, she told herself, Fred hardly ever left the Beanery except to go drinking at McGuire's speakeasy. And maybe he'd already passed through Grand Central Station, years ago. But, come to think of it, maybe her father and mother had, too. As long as she had her sign, though, which she lugged back and forth from the Hooverville every day, Annie told herself that she could keep on hoping.

But her hopes of finding her parents at Grand Central Station vanished one grey afternoon in early November. She'd already been feeling downhearted that day, thinking about winter coming on and about how – no matter how cheerful she'd try to be – the months ahead in the Hooverville would be bleak and freezing. And she'd also been worrying about how school had now been going on for over two months without her. Annie would have been in the seventh grade this fall. Instead, she was falling further and further behind in her schooling with each passing day. She'd *already* missed half of her sixth-grade year. On October 28th, her birthday had come and gone without anything special happening, for she hadn't told anyone in the Hooverville that she was twelve years old that day. So there'd been no party, or singing, or birthday kisses. But, of course, this was nothing new for Annie. Her birthday had never been celebrated at the orphanage, and she'd never in her entire life got a birthday present. All of these unhappy thoughts were going through her mind as she continued to chant, 'Apples, apples, a nickel apiece, two for a dime,' when suddenly Randy came running breathlessly up to her.

'Annie, quick, take your apples and skedaddle, there's a cop looking for you!' cried Randy. Her heart pounding with fright, Annie grabbed Sandy and ran off into the station, where she hid in a corridor not far from the entrance. A policeman. After her. Annie had never been so scared in her life. After a moment, she peeked out and saw Randy standing by the entrance talking to a policeman. The policeman was showing him a piece of paper. Randy, she saw, was shaking his head and shrugging as if to say that he knew nothing. At last, the policeman stalked angrily away, and Randy came into the station and found Annie and Sandy hiding in the corridor. 'You've got to get out of here, Annie, back to the Hooverville,' whispered Randy, pulling her further along the corridor into the shadows. 'The policeman showed me a circular with your picture on it – it says that you're wanted as a runaway orphan. He told me that he'd remembered seeing you around here – selling apples – but I told him that I hadn't seen you and that I didn't know anything about you. But then he spotted your sign and he took it away. Evidence.'

'You're right, I've got to get out of here,' Annie agreed with a shiver. And, with Sandy running at her side, she hurried through the grey afternoon to the Hooverville. That night, she and Randy and Sophie

77

decided that it would be too risky for Annie ever to go back to Grand Central Station – the police were certain to nab her. So, in the days that followed, Annie and Sandy hung around the Hooverville, helping Sophie with her cooking and going shopping with her on First Avenue. Sandy seemed to enjoy the foraging trips that they made with Sophie along the banks of the East River, to pick up pieces of driftwood for the fires they built every night in the ash cans. Being with Sophie all day was pleasant enough for Annie and Sandy, but as December came along and the weather grew sharply colder, they nearly froze in the chill afternoons as they gathered wood along the windy banks of the river. Annie grew discouraged, too – as long as she had to stay all day in the Hooverville, how could she get on with her search for her father and mother? From selling apples, Annie had saved up twenty-seven dollars, which she kept pinned in her sweater pocket, and now she decided to use the money to buy bus tickets to Florida for her and Sandy. 'As nice as the folks are to us here, we gotta be movin' on,' Annie told Sandy one night as they were lying shivering in their bed – covering themselves with even a dozen layers of newspapers just didn't seem to help much on these December nights. ' 'Cause this way I'm never gonna find my mum and dad,' Annie went on. 'We'll go down to Florida for the winter, where it's warm, and look around. Maybe they're livin' down there. Who knows? And then, if we don't find them, we'll head back up here next spring.' But it was hard for Annie to leave Sophie and Randy and all the others, to set off once again on her own. And Annie knew that, even in 1933, twenty-seven dollars wouldn't last long. 'We'll go

78

soon, maybe tomorrow, or maybe when the first snow falls,' she told Sandy, but as the December days passed, she kept postponing her departure.

Finally, it wasn't Annie who decided that her stay in the Hooverville should end. On a bitter, windy night in the middle of December, only two and a half weeks less than a year since Annie had run away from the orphanage, she and Sandy and the grown-ups were huddled around the ash-can fires when a bulky, pig-eyed police sergeant suddenly loomed up out of the shadows. 'Okay, folks, everybody outta here,' shouted the sergeant, whose name was Ward, brandishing a legal-looking document, 'we got a court order, we're tearin' down this junk pile!'

'You can't do that – this is the only home we got,' cried Sophie. 'And we're not doin' nothin' wrong here. We're not hurtin' nobody.'

'Oh, yeah, tell it to the judge,' said Sergeant Ward mockingly. He pointed to the high-rise luxury apartment houses, the dwelling places of the rich, that lined the East River above them. 'The people up there, they went to court and got this order,' he went on, 'sayin' that this here dump is an eyesore and a health hazard. And I'm only doin' my duty. So, come on, all of you bums, outta here!'

Annie stepped forward with Sandy at her side, and spoke up boldly to Sergeant Ward. 'They're not bums,' she said angrily. 'They're good, hard-workin' folks who just happen to be down on their luck. And they gotta have a place to live, too, even if they ain't rich!'

'Wait a second, you, little girl,' commanded Sergeant Ward, pointing a fat finger at Annie. 'Ain't I seen your picture on a circular at the station house? You're a runaway orphan, ain't you?'

'No, sir, I'm . . . I'm her little girl,' said Annie, pointing to Sophie.

'Oh, no, you ain't,' said Sergeant Ward, grabbing Annie by the neck of her sweater. 'You're comin' along with me. And that mutt there, he's goin' to the dog pound.'

'Oh, no, he isn't!' Annie gave Sandy a shove and called, 'Run, Sandy, run!' Sandy scampered up the embankment and, his ears flattened against his head, ran off as fast as his four legs would carry him.

'Get that dog, get that damned dog!' shouted Sergeant Ward, blowing his whistle as a squad of a dozen other policemen now appeared out of the shadows on all sides of the Hooverville. One of the policemen, waving his nightstick, ran off up the embankment after Sandy.

'Knock it down, knock down this pile junk pile!' cried Sergeant Ward to his men, still holding Annie tightly by her collar. Anne reared back and kicked him as hard as she could in the shins. 'Owww!' shrieked Sergeant Ward, letting go of Annie as he hopped about in pain. The moment that he let her go, Annie turned and ran like a streak, heading northward along the bank of the river, in the opposite direction to the one that Sandy had run.

'Get that kid, get that goddamn kid!' Sergeant Ward called after her, and Annie soon heard footsteps at her back. Behind, from the Hooverville, she heard screams and shouting and the sickening, crunching sound of the fragile, makeshift shanties being knocked down by the police. Running along the riverbank in the dark, cold night, Annie stumbled on a rock and fell. She quickly scrambled back up and ran on. But the policeman, she could hear, was gaining on her. 'I've got to run faster,' said Annie to herself, breathing heavily, ' 'cause I mustn't let him catch me. I mustn't!'

EIGHT

The following afternoon, Miss Hannigan was herding the shivering orphans into the front hallway of the orphanage after having marched them home from school. 'Come on, get in here, get in here, before you turn this place into an icebox,' she shrieked, pushing little Molly in and slamming the door shut.

'Now, get out of them sweaters and get downstairs to work,' ordered Miss Hannigan.

'Yes, Miss Hannigan,' chorused the ragamuffin gaggle of orphans as they took off their patched, threadbare sweaters and hung them up on hooks by the front door. Then they filed glumly downstairs to their sewing machines as Miss Hannigan went into her office and turned on her radio. One of Miss Hannigan's favourite soap operas, 'Ma Perkins', was just coming on. She sat down at her desk, opened the bottom drawer, removed a pint of rye whiskey, and took a long swig from it. 'Little girls,' muttered Miss Hannigan to herself, lighting a Lucky Strike cigarette and leaning back in her swivel chair to listen to the radio programme. 'Everywhere I look there's nothin' but little girls. I got all the headaches of bein' a mother and none of the advantages. Other women, they got husbands, buy 'em fur coats, take 'em out la-dee-da to the movies, but whatta I got? Little girls. I hate the sight of them. Still, there's one little girl I'd like to see again. That Annie. If I ever get her back here I'm gonna make her life so miserable she'll wish she was never born.'

Miss Hannigan must briefly have had some sinister ability to predict the future, for at the very moment that she was muttering about having Annie once again under her thumb, Annie was only a block away, being hauled roughly along the sidewalk by Sergeant Ward. 'I'm takin' you back where you belong, you little devil,' he said.

Fleeing from the policeman the night before, Annie had again stumbled over a rock, and this time she had been caught. She'd spent the night in the dank lockup of a midtown police station, in a cell with several of the Hoovervillites who'd been arrested for disturbing the peace and given thirty days in jail by a cold-hearted night-court judge. But Annie was too young to be sent to jail and was instead now being led by Sergeant Ward back to the orphanage. She'd be all right, Annie told herself, even if Miss Hannigan beat her every day, but she was worried about Sandy. He'd escaped from the policeman who was chasing him, but where was he now? Cold and hungry and homeless, without Annie to take care of him. What would become of Sandy? And how would she ever find him again? And what if he was nabbed by the dog-catcher? Then . . . Annie didn't want to think about it. Annie and Sergeant Ward had arrived in front of the orphanage. The policeman pulled the child up the steps to the front door and rang the doorbell.

'Yeah, who is it?' called Miss Hannigan, switching off

her radio and coming to the hallway to peer out the window. Hearing Miss Hannigan's hated voice again, Annie felt a chill run up her spine that had nothing to do with the blustery December wind that was blowing down St Mark's Place.

'Sergeant Ward from the Seventeenth Precinct,' said the officer as Miss Hannigan opened the door to let them in. 'We found your runaway.'

'Oh, thank you, officer,' said Miss Hannigan sweetly, flashing a false, toothy smile. 'Well, well, well, if it isn't my dear little Annie. How nice to see you again, sweetheart.' Annie edged away from Miss Hannigan and said nothing.

'We found her livin' in one of them Hoovervilles over to the river,' Sergeant Ward explained, 'with a bunch of bums.'

'They weren't bums,' muttered Annie through clenched teeth.

Sergeant Ward reached inside his jacket and took out a thin packet of money. 'She had this here twenty-seven bucks on her – probably stole it,' he said handing the packet to Miss Hannigan.

'I didn't steal it, I earned it – that's my money,' said Annie.

'Well, it's mine now, to help pay for your keep here, dear,' said Miss Hannigan, tucking the money into the front of her blouse.

'Also she had some mangy mutt with her,' Sergeant Ward went on, 'but he got away. We'll find him, though. Slap him in the dog pound.'

'I'm sure you will, officer,' agreed Miss Hannigan, putting her arm heavily around Annie's shoulder as

84

though in a gesture of affection. 'Oh, poor punkin,' she cooed, 'out in the freezin' cold with nothin' on but that thin sweater. I hope you didn't catch influenza.' Yes, thought Miss Hannigan, I hope you caught double pneumonia. 'Thanks so much again, officer,' Miss Hannigan said, smirking.

'All in the line of duty, ma'am' said Sergeant Ward, turning to glower fiercely down at Annie. 'And you. Don't let me ever hear that you run away again from this nice lady.' Sergeant Ward flicked his finger on the visor of his cap to salute Miss Hannigan. 'Good afternoon, ma'am,' he said, and off he went, out the door and down the street, leaving Annie alone in the front hallway with Miss Hannigan. At once, Miss Hannigan grabbed the girl by the scruff of her neck, dragged her into the office, and slammed the door shut behind them.

'Now . . . I'm gonna have your head,' growled Miss Hannigan in a low, menacing voice. 'And you ain't runnin' away from here ever again.' Miss Hannigan took a slow drink from her bottle of whiskey and smoothed her skirt. 'Well, missy, are you glad to be back with your Miss Hannigan? Huh?'

'Yes, Miss Hannigan.' Annie stood her ground.

'Liar!' screamed Miss Hannigan. 'What's the one thing I always taught you? Never tell a lie! Well, what's the one thing I always taught you?'

'Never tell a lie, Miss Hannigan,' Annie repeated evenly.

Miss Hannigan grabbed Annie and violently shook her. 'For what you done, runnin' away, I could get fired,' Miss Hannigan hissed. 'Have the Board of Orphans stickin' their nose in here. Well, you're gonna pay for it. I promise. You'll be sorry they caught you and brought you back here.' Miss Hannigan took down the wooden paddle that hung on the wall behind her desk and smacked it smartly across her palm. 'So, you never cry when I beat you, huh?' Miss Hannigan laughed. 'Well, this time we'll see about that.'

Outside, soon after Sergeant Ward had left the orphanage, a long black Rolls-Royce limousine turned onto St Mark's Place and glided to a halt in front of the orphanage. A uniformed chauffeur alighted from the limousine and opened the door for a beautiful blonde woman of about twenty-eight. She was wearing an elegantly cut fox-collared cashmere coat and a salmon pink hat and was carrying a slim brown calfskin briefcase. The young woman nodded to the chauffeur as she stepped out of the limousine, then gracefully climbed the front steps of the orphanage. Now, just as Miss Hannigan raised her paddle to begin beating Annie, the young woman rang the front doorbell.

'Now what?' snorted Miss Hannigan, quickly hanging up the paddle and heading for the front door. But first she turned to Annie and shoved her roughly to the floor. 'You, stay there!' she snapped. 'I'll be back to take care of you. Right away.' Miss Hannigan went to the front door and opened it a crack. 'Yeah?' she asked.

'Oh, good afternoon. Miss Hannigan, is it?' asked the young woman.

'Yeah.'

'Oh, good,' the young woman calmly continued, 'I'm

86

Miss Grace Farrell, and the New York City Board of Orphans suggested that I . . .'

'Come in, come in,' stammered Miss Hannigan. Mistaking Miss Farrell for an official of the Board of Orphans, she was terrified that she might be about to lose her job. In the Depression, where would a middle-aged spinster like herself ever find another job? Especially a job that included free room and board. So, Miss Hannigan was trembling with fright as she led Miss Farrell into her office. 'Who's this we have here?' asked Miss Farrell as she spied Annie cowering in a corner on the floor.

'Oh, that's just one of our dear little girls, Annie, who has been a very naughty little girl,' Miss Hannigan said with a false, high-pitched laugh.

'Oh, I see,' Miss Farrell murmured. 'Now, Miss Hannigan, as I was saying, the New York City Board of . . .'

'Wait. Hold it,' bridled Miss Hannigan. 'I can explain everything. It wasn't my fault. It was Annie, you see, who got into Bundles' laundry bag . . .'

'Miss Hannigan, I . . .' Miss Farrell began.

'And, sure, I know I should've informed Mr Donatelli at the Board of Orphans instead of gettin' the cops into it, but I . . .'

'Miss Hannigan, I'm sorry, but I haven't the slightest idea what you're talking about,' said Miss Farrell, casually putting her briefcase in her lap as she sat in a chair next to Miss Hannigan's desk.

Miss Hannigan suddenly changed. She looked coldly at Miss Farrell and then at her briefcase. 'Wait a minute, hold it, sister, I got it,' snarled Miss Hannigan, heaving a secret sigh of relief. 'If it's beauty products you're peddlin', you come to the wrong lady. 'Cause I don't need none. Get out!'

'Miss Hannigan, I am not "peddling" anything,' Miss Farrell calmly replied. 'I am the private secretary to Oliver Warbucks.'

'Oliver Warbucks? *The* Oliver Warbucks?' Miss Hannigan's jaw hung slackly open in astonishment.

'Yes,' said Miss Farrell. '*The* Oliver Warbucks.'

'Oh, my God!' Miss Hannigan exclaimed. 'I read in the *Daily Mirror* that Oliver Warbucks is the richest man in America. The richest man in the world!'

'Yes.' Miss Farrell was coolly matter-of-fact. 'That is more or less true.' She shifted her position slightly on the chair. 'Now, Miss Hannigan, Mr Warbucks, as a gesture of charity, has decided to invite an orphan to spend the Christmas holidays at his home. And I've been sent here to select one for him.'

'You sure he wouldn't rather have a lady?' Miss Hannigan gave a high-pitched giggle. 'I got two weeks of vacation comin'.'

Miss Farrell paid no heed to Miss Hannigan's feeble attempt at a joke as she took an official-looking document from her briefcase. Annie had been staring at Miss Farrell from the moment she entered the room. Her heart had all but stopped when she saw the beautiful blonde woman, for she was sure that it was her mother who had at last come to get her. With her shining blonde hair and beautiful face, Miss Farrell looked exactly the way Annie had always pictured her mother. But even if Miss Farrell weren't her mother,

Annie thought, she was surely the second-nicest and most lovely looking woman in the world.

'So, what sort of orphan did you have in mind?' asked Miss Hannigan, nervously pacing back and forth and stopping only to block Annie from Miss Farrell's view.

'Well, she should be friendly,' said Miss Farrell. Twisting around behind Miss Hannigan's back, Annie gave Miss Farrell a friendly little wave. Noticing the wave, Miss Farrell grinned and waved back. Miss Hannigan, starting to pace the room again, didn't see the wave or the grin or the wave back. 'And she should also be intelligent,' added Miss Farrell.

'The capital of Florida is Tallahassee,' Annie spoke up brightly. 'Capital T-a-l-l-a-h-a-s-s-e-e, Tallahassee!'

'You, shut up!' Miss Hannigan threw a murderous glance at Annie.

'And cheerful,' Miss Farrell continued. Annie laughed loudly and very cheerfully – with Miss Farrell in the same room, it was easy to be cheerful.

'I said *shut up*,' growled Miss Hannigan. 'And how old?'

'Oh, age doesn't really matter,' said Miss Farrell, leaning slightly to one side to get a better look at Annie. 'Oh, say, nine or ten.' From behind Miss Hannigan, Annie motioned upward so Miss Farrell would suggest a higher age. 'Or eleven,' Miss Farrell said. Annie kept on motioning upward. 'Or even twelve,' Miss Farrell suggested. Annie motioned for Miss Farrell to stop. 'Yes, twelve would be perfect.' Annie patted her head to indicate red hair. 'And, oh yes, I almost forgot, Mr Warbucks prefers redheaded children,' said Miss

Farrell, smiling at the little game she found herself playing with Annie behind Miss Hannigan's back. Annie leapt eagerly to her feet, but Miss Hannigan at once shoved her down again.

'Twelve? A redhead?' Miss Hannigan thought for a moment. 'No, I'm afraid we don't have any orphans like that around here.'

'Well, what about this child right here?' asked Miss Farrell, pointing to Annie, who once again popped to her feet.

'Annie? Oh, no, you wouldn't want her,' said Miss Hannigan, stepping between Annie and Miss Farrell. She was trying to think as fast as she could in her rattled state. 'You wouldn't want her because she's . . . she's a drunk! Yes, that's it. A drunk. A drunk and a liar.'

'Yes, I'm sure she's a drunk and a liar,' said Miss Farrell lightly, not for a moment believing Miss Hannigan's outrageous lies. She held out her hand to Annie. 'Annie, come here,' Miss Farrell said gently. Annie edged her way gingerly around Miss Hannigan and, smiling, went up to Miss Farrell.

'Annie, would you like to spend the next two weeks at Mr Warbucks' house?' asked Miss Farrell.

'Oh, I would love to,' breathed Annie. 'I would really love to.'

'Hold it!' snapped Miss Hannigan. 'You can have any orphan in the orphanage, but not Annie.'

'Why not?' Miss Farrell coolly asked.

'I just told you.' Miss Hannigan was losing her temper. 'She's a drunk and . . .'

Miss Farrell looked Miss Hannigan sternly in the eye.

'I assume, Miss Hannigan,' she said with authority, 'that the reason you don't want to let Annie go with me has something to do with all that business about the laundry bag and the police. Perhaps I should call Mr Donatelli at the Board of Orphans and tell him all about . . .'

'Oh, no, no, no, no – that won't be necessary,' replied Miss Hannigan with a high-pitched laugh.

Miss Farrell picked up the official-looking document that she'd taken from her briefcase and thrust it into Miss Hannigan's hands. 'Sign it,' she ordered.

'I'll sign it,' giggled Miss Hannigan, hurriedly putting her signature on the paper. The document gave Annie permission to be absent from the orphanage for two weeks under the supervision of Oliver Warbucks. 'I'm an easy gal to get along with,' Miss Hannigan said obsequiously. 'If it's Annie you want, it's Annie you get.'

'It's Annie I want,' said Miss Farrell.

'Oh, boy!' Annie exclaimed.

'Now, if you'll get her coat, I'll take her along with me right now.' Miss Farrell had her hands on Annie's shoulders.

'Coat?' Miss Hannigan rudely replied. 'Annie ain't got no coat.'

'All right,' Miss Farrell, 'then we'll buy her one.'

'Oh, boy!' Annie nearly shouted.

'We'll go to Best's and get you a nice warm winter coat,' explained Miss Farrell. 'Come along, dear. Mr Warbucks' limousine is waiting outside.

'Oh, boy!' Annie was all eyes. 'Me in a limousine. I

91

can hardly believe it.'

'*She* can hardly believe it,' muttered Miss Hannigan furiously as Miss Farrell took Annie by the hand and led her out of the office. Downstairs, through a basement window in their workroom, the orphans had seen the limousine pull up outside. Full of excitement, they'd watched the beautiful blonde woman go up to the front door and enter the orphanage. 'Maybe she's come to 'dopt one of us,' Kate had said to little Molly. 'So, if she comes down here to see us, don't forget, be pretty.' After a while, when the woman hadn't come down to the workroom, two of the orphans, Pepper and Molly, had sneaked up the stairs and tried to listen at the office door. But they could hear nothing through the thick door. They didn't know that Anne was back and in the office with Miss Hannigan and the blonde stranger. And so now, when Miss Farrell stepped out of the office with Annie, Pepper and Molly were astonished to see their old friend.

'Annie, you're back!' Molly exulted. For months, she'd been dreaming that Annie would come back to the orphanage.

'Well, yes, I'm sort of back,' said Annie hesitantly.

'What happened, the cops caught ya?' asked Pepper.

'Shh,' whispered Annie. She didn't want anyone as nice as Miss Farrell to find out that she'd been a runaway. In a low voice she told Pepper and Molly, 'Yes, they caught me, but now she's takin' me to stay in some rich man's house.' Annie knelt and gave Molly a big, warm hug. 'Don't worry, honey, I'll be back right after Christmas, and then I'll take care of you again, just like I used to,' Annie assured her. Molly was smiling and had tears in her eyes at the same time. She was too young to understand either why Annie had suddenly come back or why she was just as suddenly leaving again. For Molly, two more weeks without Annie seemed like forever.

'Okay, see ya in two weeks,' said Pepper, giving Annie an affectionate punch on the arm.

'Tell all the kids I'll be comin' back,' Annie said. 'And I'll write you from whatever this place is I'm goin' to. Merry Christmas.'

'Merry Christmas, Annie,' Molly and Pepper chorused.

'Good afternoon, Miss Hannigan,' Miss Farrell called back into the office. 'And Season's Greetings.'

'Yeah, Season's Greetin's,' absent-mindedly replied Miss Hannigan as she took out her pint of rye and finished it off in one long gulp. 'Damned Annie,' she grumbled to herself, 'goin' off to spend Christmas in the lap of luxury while I'm stuck here with a pack of rotten orphans. Well, I'll take care of her when she gets back. Good care. I'll tan her backside so's she won't be able to sit down for a month!'

Outside, the chauffeur opened the door of the limousine for Annie and Miss Farrell, and Annie found herself sitting on the plushest and most comfortable cushions she'd ever sat on, sinking down almost out of sight as Miss Farrell settled beside her. In a moment, the limousine pulled away from the kerb. Annie waved out the window of the limousine at Molly and Pepper, whose noses were pressed to the front window of the orphanage as they watched her go. Soon the limousine was headed up Fifth Avenue. 'Oh, boy,' thought Annie, taking Miss Farrell's hand and clasping it tightly, 'if Myrtle Vandenmeer could see me now.'

NINE

A few minutes later, the limousine drew to a halt in front of Best's, at Fifth Avenue and 54th Street, and Miss Farrell led Annie into the elegant department store. There she bought her the warmest and most beautiful winter coat that Annie had ever seen – it was a pale-pink wool and had a white ermine collar. And Miss Farrell also bought her a matching pink hat. Annie couldn't believe the price tags on the coat and hat – together they cost more than a hundred dollars. But Miss Farrell didn't blink an eye at the prices as she offhandedly told the saleslady, 'Charge it to Oliver Warbucks.'

Feeling like a fairy-tale princess in her new coat and hat, Annie settled luxuriously once more in the back seat of the limousine as it proceeded northward and at last stopped at the kerb in front of Oliver Warbucks' six-storey marble-pillared mansion, at Fifth Avenue and 82nd Street, across from the Metropolitan Museum of Art. The chauffeur ceremoniously opened the door, and Annie and Miss Farrell alighted from the limousine. Taking Annie by the hand, Miss Farrell led her up the steps of the mansion and rang the bell by the huge, carved-oak front door. All but instantly the door was opened by a tall, stern-faced butler in a bottle-green uniform whom Miss Farrell introduced as Drake. Now, as Drake bowed to one side, Miss Farrell led Annie into a high-ceilinged foyer that was the biggest room she'd ever seen aside from the main concourse of Grand Central Station. 'Do you really live here?' asked Annie, looking around in wide-eyed awe, 'or is this a train station?' 'We really live here,' replied Miss Farrell with a smile.

'May I take your coat and hat, miss?' Drake asked Annie. He spoke with a nasal English accent.

Annie took a wary step away from Drake. 'Will I get 'em back?' she asked.

'Of course, dear,' said Miss Farrell, smiling once again as Drake took Annie's coat and hat and tattered old sweater. Having arrived at the mansion in her beautiful new coat and hat, Annie felt embarrassed to be seen now in her patched dress and the worn-through shoes that she'd lined with cardboard during her days at the Hooverville. But neither Drake nor Miss Farrell seemed to notice how raggedy she looked in her old clothes.

Now Miss Farrell, followed by Drake, led Annie into a vast living room with a huge marble fireplace. The room, about the size of a football field, was several times larger than the foyer. A dozen or so uniformed maids and footmen were busy cleaning the room, dusting the furniture, polishing the woodwork, and vacuuming the Oriental rugs. In the centre of the room was a large statue of a naked woman who had no arms. 'What's that thing?' asked Annie, pointing at the statue.

'That's called the *Venus de Milo*, dear,' said Miss Farrell. 'There's a copy of it in a museum in Paris called the Louvre, but this one, belonging to Mr Warbucks, is the original, of course.'

'Oh,' breathed Annie.

Miss Farrell turned to Drake. 'That reminds me,' she said, 'has the new painting arrived from Paris?'

'Yes, miss,' murmured Drake, indicating a pair of servants who were unpacking a wooden crate at the far end of the living room, 'they're just setting it up now.' The servants lifted a velvet-wrapped painting out of the crate and placed it on an easel. 'Ah, good,' said Miss Farrell, 'then everything is in order for Mr Warbucks' homecoming. Has he arrived yet?'

'No, miss,' Drake replied. 'But I called Teterboro airport. His plane from Chicago landed at three-forty-five, and the car, of course, was there to pick him up. We're expecting him any minute.'

'It will be good to see Mr Warbucks again, miss,' said another of the servants, the cook, a short, plump, pleasant-faced Scottish woman named Mrs Pugh.

'Yes, six weeks is a long time,' said Miss Farrell with a sigh. Annie was surprised to notice that Miss Farrell's eyes were suddenly misty. Gee, Annie thought, she must have missed this Mr Warbucks real bad.

'Everything is ready for Mr Warbucks,' declared Mrs Pugh. 'The kitchen staff and I have prepared his favourite dinner – roast beef and Yorkshire pudding.'

'Good,' smiled Miss Farrell. 'Now, would you all come here for a moment, please?'

'Quickly, everyone; everyone, quickly,' Drake commanded, snapping his fingers as the servants lined up in a row in front of Miss Farrell and Annie.

'Everyone,' announced Miss Farrell, 'this is Annie, the orphan who will be staying with us for the next two weeks. For Christmas.'

'Miss,' the servants chorused, the women curtsying and the men bowing to Annie.

'Annie, this is . . . everyone,' said Miss Farrell.

'Hi, everyone,' said Annie with a cheery grin.

'Now, Annie,' asked Miss Farrell, 'what would you like to do first?'

Annie looked slowly around at the huge expanse of marble floors that were only partly covered by rugs and at the floor-to-ceiling windows that lined the wall of the mansion facing Fifth Avenue. 'The floors,' Annie decided. 'I'll scrub them and then I'll get to the windows.'

'Why, Annie,' Miss Farrell gasped, 'you won't have to do any work while you're here.'

'I won't?' Annie had figured that she'd been brought to the mansion at Christmastime to help do extra cleaning for the holidays. After all, everyplace she'd ever been she'd had to work for her keep.

'No, of course not,' Miss Farrell reassured her. 'You're our guest. And for the next two weeks you're going to have swell time. You'll have breakfast in bed every morning, served to you by Mrs Pugh, and Annette will make up your bed and clean your room. And then . . . well, let me see. The swimming pool is on the lower level at the rear.'

'*Inside* the house?' Annie asked.

'Yes, dear!' said Mrs Farrell.

'Oh, boy!' cried Anne.

'While you're with us, you won't lift a finger – you're

here, Annie, only to have a good time,' said Miss Farrell.

'Oh, boy,' beamed Annie, 'I think I'm gonna like it here.'

Suddenly, a loud, gruff man's voice was heard calling angrily from the foyer. 'Been away six weeks,' shouted the man. 'Where the hell is everybody?'

At once, the servants came stiffly to attention. And a moment later, the man, who was wearing a velvet-collared Chesterfield coat and a pearl-grey Homburg hat and carrying a heavy black leather briefcase, came storming into the room.

'Hello!' he boomed, slamming down his briefcase as Drake stepped forward to take the hat and coat he had angrily flung off. Frightened, Annie edged her way backward to hide behind the *Venus de Milo*. She peeked out to look at the man. He was tall, with massive shoulders, and he had a bald, totally shaven, bullet-shaped head. His eyes were piercing, ice-cold, and blue, Annie saw, and there was a dark frown on his face. All in all, he was just about the scariest-looking man that Annie had ever seen.

'Welcome home, Mr Warbucks,' said Drake.

'It's good to be home,' snapped Mr Warbucks.

'How was your flight from Chicago, sir?' Drake asked.

'Not bad,'said Mr Warbucks. 'Took eleven hours and we only had to land four times. Now, first things first. Has the painting arrived from Paris?'

Miss Farrell stepped nervously forward. 'Yes, sir, they've just uncrated it,' she said. A pair of servants scurried to the easel on which the painting had been placed and whipped off the royal-purple velvet covering. The painting was of a sweet-faced woman who was smiling slightly. Annie later learned from Miss Farrell that it was called *Mona Lisa* and that it had been painted hundreds of years ago in Italy by someone named Leonardo da Vinci. Mr Warbucks strode across the room and stood for a moment in front of the painting. 'Hmm, no, I don't think so,' he said at last. 'Ship it back to Paris, where it came from.'

'Yes, sir,' said the servants, replacing the velvet cover over the painting and starting to put it back in its crate.

'Grace?' said Mr Warbucks.

'Yes, sir.' Miss Farrell stepped forward eagerly.

'Messages?'

'Yes, sir,' said Miss Farrell. A shadow of disappointment crossed her face. For she'd been hoping that, after six weeks, he might at least have first asked her how she was. But she very efficiently got out her note pad and began reading his messages to him. 'President Roosevelt called from the White House at one-forty-eight this afternoon,' she said. 'He wants you to call him this evening.'

'Huh,' snorted Mr Warbucks, 'I'll get to *him* tomorrow. Anyone else?'

'John D. Rockefeller, Mahatma Gandhi, and Harpo Marx,' said Miss Farrell.

'Nobody important,' said Mr Warbucks. 'What did Harpo want?'

'He didn't say,' said Miss Farrell.

Mr Warbucks walked back over to the easel, where the servants were recrating the *Mona Lisa*, and motioned to them to hold it up for him to look at again. 'Hmm,' he muttered, 'maybe I could learn to live with this thing. Hang it in the upstairs back hallway.'

'Yes, sir,' said the servants.

'Drake,' snapped Mr Warbucks, turning once again to the others, 'I'll be working in my upstairs study all evening. I'll want my smoking jacket and my brown velvet trousers.'

'Yes, sir,' Drake replied.

Miss Farrell suddenly remembered Annie and spied her hiding behind the *Venus de Milo*. And now she took Annie by the hand and led her towards Mr Warbucks. Annie's heart was thumping with fear.

'Mr Warbucks,' Miss Farrell said, smiling, 'I'd like you to meet . . .'

'Oh, and Mrs Pugh,' continued Mr Warbucks, ignoring Miss Farrell and not even noticing Annie at her side.

'Yes, sir?' asked Mrs Pugh.

'I won't be having dinner tonight – I have too much back paperwork to get caught up with,' said Mr Warbucks.

'But, sir, we've prepared roast beef with Yorkshire pudding,' said Mrs Pugh, 'as a special treat for your homecoming.'

'Roast beef, huh?' said Mr Warbucks. 'No, just send up a cheese sandwich and a glass of buttermilk in a couple of hours – I haven't got time to eat.'

'Yes, sir.' Mrs Pugh curtsied.

'And, Grace, I'll need you all evening for dictation.'

'Yes, sir.'

'All right, good to see you all again,' said Mr

Warbucks brusquely to the line of servants.

'Sir,' replied the servants in unison.

'All right, Drake,' Mr Warbucks impatiently ordered, 'dismiss the staff.'

'Yes, *sir*.' Drake snapped his fingers and at once the servants quick-marched away, followed by Drake himself. Now only Mr Warbucks, Miss Farrell, and Annie were left in the room.

'Grace, if you'll get your notebook we'll get started right away,' said Mr Warbucks, picking up his briefcase and starting for the marble staircase that led from the living room to the upper floors of the mansion. Suddenly, he noticed Annie standing silently in her ragged dress. He stopped dead in his tracks, turned, and pointed at her. 'Who the hell is *that*?' he asked in an outraged bellow.

'This is Annie, Mr Warbucks,' Miss Farrell said, 'the orphan who will be spending the Christmas holidays here with us.'

'Huh?' said Mr Warbucks.

'Remember, sir, your public-relations counsel suggested that it might be a good idea for you to take in an orphaned child for the holidays – and you agreed,' Miss Farrell told him.

'Oh, yes, an orphan,' said Mr Warbucks, glowering down at Annie. 'But that's not a boy. Orphans are boys. Like Oliver Twist.'

'I'm sorry, sir, you just said "an orphan".' Miss Farrell apologized. 'And so I chose a girl.'

'Oh,' said Mr Warbucks, taken aback. 'Well, I suppose she'll have to do.' Mr Warbucks strode over to Annie and stood towering above her. 'Annie, huh?' he said. 'Annie what?'

'Sir?' said Annie, bewildered and frightened.

'What's your last name, child?'

'Oh, I'm just Annie, sir, Mr Warbucks,' Annie said. 'I haven't got any last name. That I know of.'

'So, you're just Annie, huh?'

'Just Annie,' replied Annie. 'I'm sorry that I'm not a boy.'

Mr Warbucks leaned down and put one of his huge, meaty hands on Annie's shoulder. 'Say,' he jovially asked in a sudden change of mood, 'how'd you like to meet Babe Ruth?'

'Oh, boy, sure!' cried Annie eagerly, smiling, trying to please Mr Warbucks. 'Who's Babe Ruth?'

Mr Warbucks straightened up and looked down at Annie with a sigh. 'I couldn't be happier that you'll be spending Christmas with us,' he said, patting her absently on the head and starting once again for the staircase. 'Grace,' he said, 'we'll start with the figures on the iron-ore shipments to Toledo from . . .' But then he stopped again, looking confused. Rather awkwardly, he went to Miss Farrell and hoarsely whispered, 'What the hell am I supposed to do with this child?'

'I don't know, sir,' Miss Farrell whispered in turn, 'but, well, it is her first night here.'

'It is, huh?' Mr Warbucks looked perplexed. But then he smiled a half smile and walked back to Annie. 'Well, Annie,' he said with abrupt cheerfulness, 'your first night here, I guess we ought to do something special for you. Why don't you sit down?'

'Yes, sir,' said Annie, hopping up to sit in a huge

103

maroon velvet wing chair next to the fireplace.

Mr Warbucks stood for a moment scratching his head. What the devil did one do with a little girl on an evening in New York? Suddenly, he had an idea. 'Would you like to go to a movie?' he asked.

'Gosh, sure, Mr Warbucks, I'd love to,' said Annie. And she really meant it. 'I mean, gee, I heard a lot about movies, but I've never been to one.'

'Never been to a movie?' Mr Warbucks was thunderstruck.

'No, sir,' said Annie.

'Well, then, we've got to do something about that right away,' said Mr Warbucks. All of his self-confidence had come back. 'And nothing but the best for you, Annie. You'll go to the Roxy. Then an ice-cream soda at Rumpelmayer's and a hansom cab ride around Central Park.'

'Golly!' Annie's eyes lit up with delight even though she didn't understand half of what Mr Warbucks was talking about.

'Grace, forget about the dictation for tonight,' Mr Warbucks thundered. 'We'll do it first thing in the morning. Instead, while I'm working you take Annie out to the movies.'

'Yes, sir,' said Miss Farrell.

'Aw, gee,' said Annie disappointedly.

'Is something the matter, Annie?' asked Mr Warbucks.

'Oh, no, nothing, sir,' replied Annie. 'It's just that . . . aw, gee.'

'No, what is it, child?' asked Mr Watbucks. 'You don't want to go to the Roxy?'

'Oh, no. I want to go,' said Annie. 'It's just that, well . . . I thought you were going to take me.'

'*Me*?' said Mr Warbucks, flabbergasted. 'No, no, I'm afraid I'll be far too busy tonight to . . .'

'Awwww, gee,' said Annie.

'You see, Annie, I've just been away for six weeks,' explained Mr Warbucks, 'making an inspection tour of my factories. Or what's left of my factories, with this damn Depression. And when a man is running a multi-billion-dollar corporation he doesn't have time . . .'

'Oh, sure, Mr Warbucks, I know all about it,' said Annie. 'And, heck, if you don't want to take a little girl from an orphanage to the movies, that's okay.'

'Well, now, I wouldn't put it that way,' said Mr Warbucks. The phone rang and Miss Farrell answered it.

'Excuse me, sir,' she said, holding out the phone to Mr Warbucks, 'Bernard Baruch is calling.' In 1933, Bernard Baruch was – aside from Oliver Warbucks – the wealthiest and most powerful financier in America. And he was also a close friend and adviser to President Franklin D. Roosevelt. But Annie, of course, had never heard of Bernard Baruch and had no idea whom Mr Warbucks was now talking to on the phone.

'Hello, Barney!' bellowed Mr Warbucks. Annie got up from her chair and came to stand beside him, staring pleadingly up at him with eyes that said, 'Please, come to the movies with me.' 'Yes, I just got in a couple of hours ago,' Mr Warbucks continued into the phone. 'No, I didn't get to Cleveland. But I was in Detroit and Chicago. And, Barney, I didn't like what I saw out there. Factories shut down. *My* factories shut down . . . You're darn tootin', if I'm not making money, nobody is. And damn it. Barney, your pal Roosevelt has got to do something drastic. He's got to come up with a new approach, a new plan, a new . . . something.' Unnerved by Annie's unblinking eyes, Mr Warbucks, still holding the telephone, edged away from her. But Annie stepped resolutely forward to stand once again in front of him. 'Yes, I know that Roosevelt is a Democrat, but he's a human being, too,' Mr Warbucks went on. 'Yes, I'll talk to you about it. Come over here tonight . . . Good, we'll be able to . . . I can show you all the figures on . . .' Mr Warbucks looked down at Annie. She looked soulfully back up at him. He heaved a great sigh of defeat. 'Look, Barney,' he said into the phone, 'we better make it sometime tomorrow. Tonight . . . tonight, I forgot, I've got a date to go the movies. With an eleven-year-old girl.'

Annie stood up on her tiptoes and whispered into his ear. 'I'm twelve,' she said.

'I was mistaken, Barney, she's twelve,' said Mr Warbucks. 'Good-bye, Barney.'

Mr Warbucks hung up the phone and gazed down at Annie with a shake of his head and just slightest hint of a smile. 'Okay, kiddo, you win.' He went to the archway leading to the foyer and called out, 'Drake!'

'Yes, sir?'

'Coats. For Miss Farrell, Miss Annie, and me!'

'Yes, sir,' Drake came into the living room with the coats all but instantly.

'We're going out to the movies, Drake,' said Mr Warbucks, getting into his Chesterfield.

'Yes, sir,' said Drake as he helped Annie on with her coat. 'Will you be wanting the Rolls-Royce or the Dusenberg, sir?'

'The Dusenberg,' replied Mr Warbucks. 'No, wait, This child has been cooped up in an orphanage. We won't drive, we'll walk.'

'*Walk* to the Roxy?' said Miss Farrell.

'Sure, why not?' said Mr Warbucks, gaily swinging his green silk scarf around his neck. 'It's only forty-five blocks.'

'Yes, sir!' smiled Miss Farrell, looking surprised but happy.

A few moments later, bundled up warmly in their coats, hats, and scarves, Mr Warbucks, Miss Farrell, and Annie stepped out the front door of the mansion into the cold but clear and starry New York night.

'Ah, smell that,' said Mr Warbucks, taking a deep breath of the city air, 'Fifth Avenue bus fumes. There is no air like the air of New York. And you don't realize how much you miss it – the whole damn city – until you've been away from it for a while. Like the man says, "After New York, everyplace else is Bridgeport".'

And soon, as warm as cinnamon toast in her beautiful new pink wool coat and hat, Annie found herself strolling down Fifth Avenue hand in hand with Grace Farrell, who – aside from her mother, whom she hadn't yet met – was clearly the prettiest and nicest woman in the whole world, and with Mr Oliver Warbucks, who not only was the richest man in the world but who also seemed pretty nice, too. For a kid from an orphanage

107

who spent last night in jail, I'm not doing bad for myself, thought Annie, smiling to herself – so this is what it's like to be happy.

TEN

Annie would never forget her night on the town with Mr Warbucks and Miss Farrell. She was dazzled by the Roxy Theatre, with its vaulted ceilings, mirrors, murals, and dark-red carpets. And she was even more dazzled by the movie at the Roxy, *Little Women*, starring Katharine Hepburn. She laughed and cried at *Little Women*, while all the time munching happily away at the hot buttered popcorn and Hershey bars with almonds that Mr Warbucks had bought for her. 'Gee, I love movies – I want to see every movie they ever made,' said Annie, starry-eyed, as the three of them came out of the Roxy to find Mr Warbucks' Rolls-Royce limousine waiting for them at the kerb. 'From now on, Annie, you'll get to see all of the movies you want,' promised Mr Warbucks.

The climbed into the limousine and drove to Rumpelmayer's, on Central Park South, where Mr Warbucks treated Annie to the biggest chocolate ice-cream soda she'd ever set eyes on. And then, bundled up in blankets against the cold of the December night, they took a ride around Central Park in a horse-drawn hansom cab. On the way home to Mr Warbucks' mansion, Annie fell asleep in the back of the limousine. And Mr Warbucks, she later vaguely remembered, carried her upstairs and put her to bed in a bigger and more comfortable bed than she'd ever imagined even existed. Half awake when he tucked her into the bed, Annie smiled up at Mr Warbucks and then fell asleep again, remembering as her eyes grew heavy that only the night before she'd slept on the cement floor of a police station-house cell. 'I guess that's the best thing about life,' whispered Annie to herself as she drifted downward into sleep, 'you never know what's going to happen next.'

The following morning, Annie was awakened at ten o'clock by a gentle knocking at her bedroom door. It was the cook, Mrs Pugh, bringing her breakfast in bed. Annie had never before slept so late as ten o'clock, and, of course, she'd also never before had breakfast in bed. The breakfast was delicious. A large glass of freshly squeezed orange juice, an enormous stack of pancakes soaked in Log Cabin maple syrup, two poached eggs, hot buttered toast, strawberry jam, a glass of milk, and a cup of hot chocolate. 'I could get used to this, real easy,' smiled Annie to herself, wiping jam from her face with an Irish-linen napkin.

After breakfast, a pair of French maids. Annette and Cécille, helped her to bathe and then to dress in a lavender-and-white organdie dress and a pair of black patent-leather shoes that Miss Farrell had bought for her that morning at Best's. Gosh, thought Annie, I'm better dressed now than Myrtle Vandenmeer. Miss Farrell had also bought her six other dresses and four more pairs of shoes. 'I didn't know that anybody ever had more than one pair of shoes at a time,' remarked Annie to Annette and Cécille as they brushed and combed her hair. When she was ready to go downstairs,

Annie looked at herself in the full-length mirror that hung on her bedroom wall. 'Golly, get a load of me!' she exclaimed. Her bedroom, which was dominated by the outsized canopy bed in which she'd slept the night before under salmon-pink silk sheets, was decorated in various shades of pink – there were pink drapes, a pink carpet, and pale-pink flowered wallpaper. It was the most beautiful – and the pinkest – room that Annie had ever seen.

That afternoon, after a scrumptious lunch of baked ham, sweet potatoes, hot biscuits, and apple pie, Annie went swimming with Miss Farrell in the mansion's indoor pool. In a light-blue bathing suit that Miss Farrell had picked up for her at Lord & Taylor, Annie splashed happily about at the shallow end of the huge pool. She'd never been in a pool before, and, of course, she didn't know how to swim. 'We'll do something about that right away,' said Miss Farrell, and within an hour an instructor – a man named Johnny Weissmuller, who had been a gold-medal winner in swimming for the United States in the 1932 Olympics – arrived to teach Annie to swim. Annie was a fast learner, and by the end of the afternoon she was able to float and to swim a couple of tentative strokes. 'I wish I could give you more lessons – you'd be an Olympic swimmer in no time,' beamed Mr Weissmuller, 'but I'm off tomorrow to Hollywood to play the title role in a movie version of *Tarzan*.' 'I'll go to see you in it, Mr Weissmuller, I promise,' said Annie.

That evening, Mr Warbucks took Annie out to dinner in the Peacock Alley room of the Waldorf Astoria Hotel, where they dined on caviar, which Annie didn't especially like, pheasant under glass, and an incredibly delicious dessert called Baked Alaska. Mr Warbucks told Annie that he, too, had enjoyed their night out together at the Roxy. 'You know, Annie,' he mused, sipping on a glass of Mumm's champagne, 'I haven't taken a vacation in years. Been too busy. But now, damn it, for the next two weeks, while you're visiting, I'm going to take one. To hell with work – for once, I'll let my business take care of itself. I'm going to show you New York like no one has ever seen it.'

At the age of fifty-two, Mr Warbucks was a self-made billionaire whose entire life was devoted to work. Indeed, although he had kept company with some of the most beautiful women in the world, including Gloria Swanson and Mary Pickford and Greta Garbo, he had never married. He'd been too absorbed in building up a financial empire that encompassed everything from oil wells in Oklahoma to automobile factories in Detroit to rubber plantations in Brazil. He was the world's richest man, but was also perhaps the world's loneliest man. For he had no family and virtually no friends. And he almost never took a day off from work. Until now.

In the next days, Mr Warbucks kept his promise to show New York to Annie. He took her everywhere – to the Stock Exchange, to the Statue of Liberty, to St Patrick's Cathedral, to the Bronx Zoo, to Radio City Music Hall, and to the top of the Empire State Building. 'Gee, to think that I lived here all of my life and never saw any of these things,' exclaimed Annie as Mr Warbucks pointed out the sights to her from an airplane he'd chartered to fly her over the city. And they saw at least one movie every day, everything from Shirley Temple in *Little Miss Marker* to the Marx Brothers in *Duck Soup*.

As they roamed the city together, hand in hand, the tall shaven-headed man and the little redheaded girl, Annie told Mr Warbucks about her life at the orphanage. 'That Miss Hannigan should be horse-whipped,' said Mr Warbucks, making a mental note to have one of his aides contact the Board of Orphans and have them investigate Miss Hannigan. Annie also told him about her stay at Bixby's Beanery. 'That couple violated the child-labour laws, making you work like that,' said Mr Warbucks angrily. 'One phone call and I can have that place shut down and Fred and Gert Bixby thrown into jail.'

'Oh, no, Mr Warbucks, please, don't do that,' begged Annie. 'They didn't mean any real harm – they're just kind of stupid people.'

'All right, I won't,' said Mr Warbucks. 'But you're a lot more forgiving than I am, Annie.'

One afternoon, as she and Mr Warbucks chanced to stroll by Grand Central Station, Annie pointed out the place where she'd sold apples and told him about her life in the Hooverville. She recalled how everyone there – especially Randy and Sophie – had been so kind to her. And, finally, she told Mr Warbucks about her dog, Sandy. 'Annie, I doubt if there's any chance of your ever finding Sandy again, assuming that he's still alive,' said Mr Warbucks bluntly. 'But I'll do everything in my power to help you find him.' And, within twenty-four hours, Mr Warbucks had hired a dozen of the best

113

detectives from the best private-detective agency in New York, Pinkerton's, and set them to searching the city for Sandy.

'If he's to be found, the Pinkertons will find him,' promised Mr Warbucks, and each night before she went to bed, Annie got down on her knees and prayed that the private detectives would find Sandy, safe and sound. Once a day, Annie wrote a letter to the children at the orphanage, telling them about her adventures as Mr Warbucks' holiday guest. She wrote them that Mr Warbucks had Pinkertons out looking for Sandy.

'What's a Pinkerton?' asked Molly as Pepper was reading Annie's latest letter aloud to the orphans. 'You dope, everybody knows that,' said Pepper. 'They're another kind of dog, like bloodhounds – it takes one to find one.'

'Oh,' said Molly.

One evening, a few days after Annie had come to stay at the mansion, Mr Warbucks summoned Miss Farrell to his upstairs study. 'Grace,' he said, turning red with embarrassment, 'I've decided . . . uh, I've decided that . . . I want to adopt Annie.'

'Oh, Mr Warbucks, how wonderful!' exclaimed Miss Farrell.

'Of course it's not that I personally care anything about her,' said Mr Warbucks, trying to cover his embarrassment by being gruff, 'but, well, I wouldn't want that poor kid to have to go back to that damned orphanage again. And we've got plenty of extra room here. Besides, I mean, she's a hell of a nice little girl, isn't she?'

'Yes, sir, she certainly is,' agreed Miss Farrell with a radiant smile. Mr Warbucks' attempt to hide his feelings for Annie was not fooling her for a moment.

'All right, first thing tomorrow morning, contact my attorney, Morris Ernst, and have him draw up the necessary adoption papers,' commanded Mr Warbucks.

'Yes, sir!' Miss Farrell cried happily. 'And I'll also go to the Board of Orphans and have them draw up the papers releasing Annie from Miss Hannigan's care.'

'Good,' said Mr Warbucks. 'The sooner that Annie never has to have anything to do with that woman ever again, the better.'

'I couldn't agree more, sir!'

The following morning, Miss Farrell paid calls at the offices of Mr Ernst and the Board of Orphans, and by noontime, with the appropriate legal papers tucked in her briefcase, she arrived at the front door of the orphanage. Miss Farrell wasn't at all malicious or vindictive, but, having learned all about Miss Hannigan from Annie, she couldn't help being eager to see the expression on Miss Hannigan's face when she found out that Annie was going to be adopted by Oliver Warbucks. So, although she could just as easily have broken the news to Miss Hannigan by letter or over the phone, instead she went to the orphanage in person. The orphans were in school when she got there and Miss Hannigan was alone in her office, where she'd just turned on the radio to another of her favourite soap operas, 'The Romance of Helen Trent'. 'Once again, we bring you "The Romance of Helen Trent",' intoned the radio announcer in a deep, syrupy voice as the strains of the programme's theme song, 'Juanita', were heard on an organ in the background. 'The story of a woman who sets out to prove for herself what so many women long to prove. That because a woman is thirty-five, or more, romance in life need not be over. That romance can live on in life at thirty-five, or after.'

'Oh, merciful God, I hope so,' groaned Miss Hannigan, taking a swig from her pint of rye whiskey and lighting up a Lucky Strike cigarette. The best thing that had happened in years to Miss Hannigan was that – three weeks earlier – Prohibition had been repealed. And so now she could buy whiskey legally and cheaply in liquor stores instead of from high-priced bootleggers. Now in fact, she could afford to be drunk from early morning until night. 'Oh, damn, who the hell is that?' muttered Miss Hannigan angrily as Miss Farrell rang the front doorbell. Miss Hannigan switched off the radio, slipped the pint of rye into a desk drawer, and went to the front door.

'Good afternoon, Miss Hannigan,' Miss Farrell said brightly as the door was opened.

'Well, well, well, if it ain't Farrell,' said Miss Hannigan, leading Miss Farrell into her office. 'You're early. Only one week. What'sa matter, Warbucks fed up with Annie already? You come to tell me she's comin' back before Christmas?'

'Oh, no, no, on the contrary, Miss Hannigan,' smiled Miss Farrell, settling gracefully into a chair next to Miss Hannigan's desk. '*Mr* Warbucks is delighted with

116

Annie. And Annie is having the time of her life.'

'How nice,' said Miss Hannigan, taking a drag on her cigarette.

'Yes, she and Mr Warbucks are practically inseparable,' Miss Farrell continued. 'They go everywhere together. To the Roxy, to the Stock Exchange, and, oh, guess where they had lunch yesterday?'

'The Waldorf?'

'No, the Automat.'

'The Automat,' grunted Miss Hannigan. 'Slummin', huh?'

Miss Farrell opened her briefcase and took out a pale-blue legal document. 'Miss Hannigan, I know that you're terribly busy, as always,' said Miss Farrell, handing her the papers, 'but this has to be signed by you and sent back to Mr Donatelli at the Board of Orphans by no later than ten o'clock tomorrow morning.'

'Huh, what is this?' asked Miss Hannigan, looking in puzzlement at the document.

'This is a release – releasing Annie from your care and from the care of the Board of Orphans,' Miss Farrell explained.

'A release?' Miss Hannigan looked confused. 'I don't get it.'

'You will,' said Miss Farrell coolly. 'Because, you see, Mr Warbucks is so taken with Annie that . . . guess what?'

'What?' asked Miss Hannigan.

'He has decided to adopt her,' announced Miss Farrell with a smile.

Miss Hannigan's jaw suddenly dropped so wide open that her teeth all but fell out. And her cigarette did indeed fall from her mouth to the floor, where she clumsily stamped it out. But she tried otherwise to remain outwardly unbothered by the news of Annie's good fortune. 'How nice,' said Miss Hannigan, sitting down dazedly behind her desk. 'How wonderful. Now, let me get this wonderful news straight. Annie is gonna be Warbucks' kid? The daughter of a millionaire?'

'Oh, no, no, no,' chuckled Miss Farrell. 'He's not a millionaire.'

'He isn't?' said Miss Hannigan.

'No, he's a billionaire,' said Miss Farrell.

'A billionaire,' repeated Miss Hannigan, shaking her head in disbelief.

'And so I've dropped by here today, in person, to tell you that Annie won't be coming back here to the orphanage,' Miss Farrell went on. 'Ever.'

'Ever,' Miss Hannigan said. 'My, my, my, my.' Miss Hannigan got to her feet uncertainly. 'Would you excuse me for a minute, please?' she asked.

'Of course,' replied Miss Farrell, grinning to herself as Miss Hannigan stepped out of the office, closed the door behind her, and went into the front hallway. From the office, Miss Farrell now heard Miss Hannigan let out the longest and loudest scream she'd ever heard. It was a scream of envy and frustration and rage that Annie not only had gotten away from her but also was about to become the richest child in the world. After a few moments, pulling herself together, Miss Hannigan came calmly back into the office and sat down again behind her desk. She stared glassy-eyed at Miss

Farrell. 'You got any more wonderful news for me?' she asked.

'No, I believe that's all the wonderful news for today,' said Miss Farrell, snapping her briefcase shut and rising. 'So good day, Miss Hannigan.'

'Yeah, good day,' mumbled Miss Hannigan.

'Oh, and Merry Christmas,' added Miss Farrell.

'Yeah, Merry Christmas,' Miss Hannigan muttered. The minute that Miss Farrell left her office, she took out her pint of whiskey and finished it off in one long swig.

Outside in the hallway, as she was turning from the office towards the front door, Miss Farrell bumped into a tall unshaven hatchet-faced man in a battered tan fedora and a shabby brown pinstriped suit. With him was a heavily made-up bleached-blonde woman of about twenty-five in a ratty fox-fur coat. 'Oops, pardon me, blondie,' the man said with a wink at Miss Farrell. And then, as though attempting to be funny, he flapped his arms and loudly crowed like a rooster. Miss Farrell looked at the man and the woman with horror and quickly made her way out to Mr Warbucks' waiting limousine.

As the limousine drove off down St Mark's Place, the man shoved open Miss Hannigan's office door and sidled into the room. A cigarette dangled from one corner of his mouth, and his narrow dark eyes were hard and cruel-looking. 'Hi ya, Sis,' he said to Miss Hannigan in a smooth, oily voice. 'Long time no see.'

'Rooster? Oh, my God, it never rains but it pours,' said Miss Hannigan as she got up with a sigh from her desk. The man was her younger brother, Rooster Hannigan, whom she hadn't seen in years. The last she'd heard of him, he was serving a jail sentence up the Hudson River, in Sing Sing. 'They finally let you outta the Big House?'

'Yeah, I got six months off for good behaviour,' bragged Rooster.

'I'll bet – what were you in for this time?' asked Miss Hannigan. Rooster had been in jail off and on since he was fourteen years old, when he'd been picked up for robbing a delicatessen on lower Second Avenue. He was forty-three now and a confirmed criminal who made a marginal living for himself by pretending to be a stockbroker and selling phony gold-mining certificates to gullible victims, mainly aged widows.

'Ahh, some dumb old dame from Yonkers claimed I swindled her outta eleven hundred bucks,' grumbled Rooster.

'Oh, yeah, and why'd she say that?' Miss Hannigan asked.

'Because Rooster swindled her outta eleven hundred bucks,' drawled the bleached-blonde young woman. Miss Hannigan disdainfully looked her up and down. I should have known, she thought, Rooster never turns up anywhere without some cheap floozy in tow.

'Ah, Lily,' said Rooster. 'Sis, I'd like you to meet a friend of mine from, uh . . .'

'Jersey City,' supplied Lily.

'Oh, yeah, Jersey City,' said Rooster. 'Miss Lily St Regis.'

Lily wriggled hippily across the room, plumped down in the chair next to Miss Hannigan's desk, and

120

crossed her legs. 'I'm named after the hotel,' she explained in a deep, throaty voice, sounding like a bad imitation of Mae West.

Miss Hannigan scowled at Lily with undisguised hatred in her eyes. 'Which floor?' she asked sarcastically.

'Don't you just love Lily, Sis?' said Rooster. He could see that the two women clearly loathed each other at first sight.

'Yeah, I'm nuts about her,' Miss Hannigan spat out. 'Rooster, do me a favour – get outta here and take the St Regis with you.'

'Aw, c'mon, Sis, give us a break,' Rooster begged.

'Can it,' Miss Hannigan snarled. 'Lookin' for another handout, huh?'

'Nah, I got eighty bucks comin' in the mail, Thursday,' Rooster lied. 'So's all I need is ten bucks to tide me over. I'll pay you back Friday, double, twenty bucks.'

'Uh-uh,' said Miss Hannigan. 'Not even a nickel for the subway, Rooster.'

'Five bucks, Aggie,' pleaded Rooster.

'Ha, I gotta laugh,' chuckled Miss Hannigan. 'Five bucks. You, with all your big deals and big talk. You was gonna be livin' in clover.'

'Oh, yeah, what about you?' Rooster retorted. 'This place ain't exactly Buckingham Palace.'

'Oh, yeah, I'm on the city,' Miss Hannigan answered defensively. 'Steady salary, free eats, free room, free gas and electric. I'm doin' all right.'

'Sis, let's face it,' said Rooster, putting his arm about his sister's shoulder, 'you're doin' like I'm doin'.'

121

'Lousy,' Lily suddenly spoke up.

'Aw, Aggie, how'd the two Hannigan kids ever end up like this?' Rooster asked. 'On the skids.'

'I'm *not* on the skids – I'm doin' okay,' Miss Hannigan insisted, unwilling to admit that her life was empty and bitter. But Miss Hannigan and her brother had never had much of a chance in life. They'd grown up in a fifth-floor walk-up cold-water flat in a slum tenement on Rivington Street, on the Lower East Side of Manhattan. Their mother had been a drunkard who'd spent most of her days sitting glassy-eyed in saloons and their father had been a small-time gambler who'd been in constant trouble with the police. Both parents had died when the children were teen-agers. Rooster had gone off to jail, and for a time young Agatha Hannigan had made a living for herself as a clerk in a grocery store. And then, when she was twenty-three, she'd had a piece of good luck. Her mother's older brother, Uncle Joe, was a member of Tammany, the Democratic political club that ran New York in those days, and for a hundred-dollar bribe Uncle Joe used his influence at City Hall to get Miss Hannigan the job as headmistress of the orphanage. And she'd had the job now for over twenty-three years.

Having had no luck in borrowing money from his sister, Rooster now quickly tried to figure out another way to get his hands on some cash. 'Say Aggie,' he asked, 'who was the blondie I bumped into when I came in here? She looked like she had a couple of bucks she might want to lend to a nice guy like me.'

'She works for Oliver Warbucks,' Miss Hannigan told him.

122

'*The* Oliver Warbucks?' Lily asked in astonishment. 'The millionaire?'

'No, the billionaire,' Miss Hannigan coolly replied. 'You dumb . . . hotel. She works for him in his mansion up on Fifth Avenue.'

'Fifth Avenue?' said Rooster with a scornful laugh. 'He don't live on Fifth Avenue.'

'He don't?' asked Miss Hannigan with surprise. 'Where does he live?'

'He lives on Easy Street,' answered Rooster, his eyes narrowing with envy, 'where all of the rich guys live – sleep 'til noon, clip coupons, and never do a lick of work. And Easy Street, Sis, that's where yours truly, Daniel Francis Hannigan, is headed for.'

'Yeah, I'll bet,' Miss Hannigan scoffed.

'Listen, Sis, what did that blonde dame want here?' Rooster asked.

'She brought me the wonderful news that one of the orphans from here, Annie – oh, God, how I hate that miserable kid – is gettin' adopted by Warbucks,' said Miss Hannigan bitterly. 'She's gonna have everything. That rotten orphan is gonna have everything.'

'Crummy orphan, livin' in the lap of luxury, it ain't fair,' said Lily.

'No, it ain't fair,' Rooster agreed. 'But listen, Sis, if an orphan from here is that close to big-time dough, there's gotta be a way we can cut ourselves in for a piece of it.'

'Yeah, sure, but how?' asked Miss Hannigan.

'I don't know . . . yet,' replied Rooster with a sinister grin. 'But there's gotta be a way. Gotta be. And I'll think of one. Even if we have to, you know, kidnap this Annie and knock her off.'

Now, Miss Hannigan, Rooster, and Lily huddled together, whispering, trying to come up with a plan to make money for themselves out of Annie's involvement with Oliver Warbucks. And although Annie had no way of knowing it as she swam in Mr Warbucks' pool, her life was suddenly and frighteningly in danger.

ELEVEN

Later that afternoon, in his Fifth Avenue mansion, Mr Warbucks was talking on the telephone with President Roosevelt in Washington when Miss Farrell came into his oak-panelled study to report on her progress in arranging for Annie's adoption. He was holding the telephone away from his ear, because President Roosevelt seemed to be doing all the talking. 'Yakety yakety yak,' whispered Mr Warbucks to Miss Farrell as President Roosevelt talked on and on.

'Yes . . . yes, Mr President,' said Mr Warbucks into the phone, at last getting a chance to speak, 'I'll grant you that Barney Baruch and I are not exactly standing on breadlines. Yet . . . No, I am not asking for you help! I've never asked for any man's help and I never will!' Mr Warbucks was furious at President Roosevelt's suggestion that Oliver Warbucks would ask for anyone's help, for he took immense pride in being a self-made man who had battled his way to the top entirely on his own. 'Listen, Mr President,' Mr Warbucks heatedly went on, 'I'm telling you that you've got to do something about what's going on in this country and do it damned fast! All right, we'll talk about it further when I come down to the White House on Wednesday.' Miss Farrell whispered to Mr Warbucks that he should perhaps be a little friendlier to the President. Mr

Warbucks shrugged, sighed, and then said into the phone. 'I'll tell you Mr President, why don't the two of us bury the hatchet? And you come here for supper on Christmas Eve on your way to Hyde Park. Wonderful. Good-bye, Mr President.'

Mr Warbucks hung up the phone and frowned. 'If I'd thought he was going to say yes I never would have asked him,' he complained. 'Grace, call Al Smith and find out what Democrats eat.'

'Yes, sir,' nodded Miss Farrell.

'Oh, and take a note,' Mr Warbucks added. 'Wednesday morning, at eleven a.m., I have a meeting at the White House with President Roosevelt and his Cabinet.'

'Yes, sir,' said Miss Farrell, handing him the adoption papers that his lawyers had drawn up and explaining that the signed release from the orphanage would be placed on file at the Board of Orphans the following morning. 'Everything is in order, sir,' she went on. 'There's nothing standing in the way now of your adopting Annie – these papers simply have to be signed by you and a judge and she's legally your daughter.'

'Good,' Mr Warbucks said. 'Good work, Grace. Now, has the package from Tiffany's arrived yet?'

'Yes, sir,' answered Miss Farrell, handing him a small package wrapped in blue-green paper and tied with a red ribbon. 'It got here just few minutes ago.'

'Good,' said Mr Warbucks, nervously hefting the package in his hands. 'I'm going to give her this thing and then tell her that I want to adopt her. Where is Annie?'

'She's in her bedroom, sir, writing another letter to her friends at the orphanage,' Miss Farrell said. 'I'll go get her.'

'Fine,' murmured Mr Warbucks, suddenly looking shaky and unsure of himself, not at all like one of the most powerful men in America. 'Damn, what's come over me?'

'You don't have to be nervous, sir,' soothed Miss Farrell. Tears glistened in her eyes, for she was moved to see her coldhearted employer looking so vulnerable and uncertain. For years, Miss Farrell had been secretly in love with Mr Warbucks and had always sensed that, beneath his tough exterior, he was a warm and kind man. And she wanted to weep with joy now at the discovery that what she'd always felt about him was really true. 'Annie is going to be the happiest little girl in the world when you tell her the news,' she sang out.

'You're damned right she is,' growled Mr Warbucks, returning to his usual gruff manner, 'and I'm not nervous. Now, get her in here.'

'Yes, sir,' said Miss Farrell with a smile, and a minute later she led Annie, who was wearing a pale-blue velvet dress and white patent-leather shoes, into the study. 'I'll . . . I'll leave you two alone,' said Miss Farrell, stepping from the study and closing the door behind her.

'Hello, Annie, how are you this afternoon?' Mr Warbucks asked cheerfully.

'Fine, thank you,' Annie replied nervously. She wasn't exactly sure what Mr Warbucks wanted to see her about, but she was certain that it was something bad. It had never been good news when she'd been called into Miss Hannigan's office at the orphanage. 'How are you, sir?'

'Fine,' Mr Warbucks answered, 'fine.' With his hands trembling slightly, Mr Warbucks picked up the adoption papers from his desk. 'Annie,' he began, 'the time has come for the two of us to have a very serious discussion.'

'Oh, it's okay, you're sending me back to the orphanage before Christmas, right?' asked Annie.

'Of course not,' Mr Warbucks assured her, taken aback that she'd even think such a thing. 'Annie, can we have a man-to-man talk?'

'Sure,' said Annie, sitting down in a large brown leather chair next to Mr Warbucks' mahogany desk.

'Annie, before we go any further, I think you should know a few things about me,' said Mr Warbucks, nervously clearing his throat and beginning to pace about the room as he spoke. 'I was born into a very poor family in what they call Hell's Kitchen, right here in New York. Both of my parents died before I was ten. And I made a promise to myself – some day, one way or another, I was going to be rich. Very rich.'

'That was a good idea,' Annie gravely observed.

'By the time I was twenty-three I'd made my first million,' Mr Warbucks went on. 'Then, in ten years, I turned that million into a hundred million dollars.' Mr Warbucks stopped, shook his head, and sighed at the memory of the vast fortune he'd amassed at so young an age. 'And in those days that was a lot of money,' he continued. 'Anyway, making money is all I've ever given a damn about. And I might as well tell you, Annie, I was ruthless to those I had to climb over to get to the

128

top. Because I've always believed one thing: you don't have to be nice to the right people you meet on the way up if you're not coming back down again. But lately, since you came to stay here, I've realized something. No matter how many Rembrandt's or Rolls-Royces you've got, if you have no one to share your life with, if you're alone, then you might as well be broke and back in Hell's Kitchen. Annie, do you understand what I'm trying to say?'

'Sure,' chirped Annie, who in fact wasn't sure at all.

'Good,' said Mr Warbucks.

'Kind of,' Annie said hesitantly.

'Kind of?' asked Mr Warbucks.

'I guess not,' admitted Annie.

'Damn!' Mr Warbucks exclaimed. It had been most painful for him to bare his feelings to Annie, and now all that he'd said had come to nothing. He looked around, spied the package from Tiffany's on his desk, and picked it up. 'I was in Tiffany's yesterday and picked up this thing for you,' he said, handing the package to Annie. 'I had it engraved.'

'For me?' asked Annie, unwrapping the small package. 'Gee, thanks, Mr Warbucks. You're so nice to me all of the time.' Annie opened the Tiffany box and saw that it contained a silver locket. 'Oh, gee,' she said in a small voice, obviously unhappy about the present.

'It's a silver locket, Annie,' Mr Warbucks explained. 'I noticed that old, broken one you always wear, and I said to myself, I'm going to get that kid a nice shiny new locket.'

'Gee, thanks, Mr Warbucks,' said Annie, trying to sound pleased about the gift but not succeeding very

129

well. 'Thank you very much.'

Mr Warbucks stepped around behind Annie and reached for the clasp of her old locket. 'Here,' he said. 'we'll just take this old one off and . . .'

'*No!*' cried Annie, leaping to her feet and backing away from Mr Warbucks. 'Please, don't make me take my locket off. I don't want a new one!'

'Annie, what is it?' asked Mr Warbucks, stunned by her unexpected reaction to his gift.

'This locket,' began Annie, fingering the cherished locket that she'd worn all her life, 'my mum and dad left it with me when . . . when they left me at the orphanage.' She was struggling not to cry. 'And there was a note, too! They're comin' back for me. And, oh, I know I'm real lucky, bein' here with you for Christmas, but . . .' Tears began to stream down Annie's cheeks, and for the first time that she could ever remember, she was crying. 'But . . . I don't know how to say it,' Annie went on, sobbing, her face wet with tears, 'the one thing I want in all the world . . . more than anything else, is to find my mother and father. And to be like other kids, with folks of my own!'

From the next room, Miss Farrell had heard Annie shouting and crying, and now, as she came into the study to investigate, Annie went running to her and, sobbing, buried herself in Miss Farrell's arms.

'Annie . . . Annie, it'll be all right,' said Mr Warbucks, dazed and nearly heartbroken to discover that Annie preferred her unknown parents to him. 'I'll find them for you. I'll find your parents for you.'

'Shh, shh, baby, it's going to be all right,' said Miss Farrell consolingly. She held Annie tightly in her arms

130

and stroked the child's hair as Annie continued to cry and cry.

Mr Warbucks, feeling foolish and unwanted, stood helplessly in the middle of the room. 'I'll . . . I'll get her a brandy,' he murmured, and rushed out of the room with a glint of tears in his eyes.

After several minutes, Annie at last stopped crying. She stepped away from Miss Farrell, rubbed her tear-reddened eyes, and sadly smiled. 'I'm sorry,' she said.

'There's nothing to be sorry about, dear – you're allowed to cry, too, like other children,' said Miss Farrell. 'But from now on you'll have nothing to cry about. Because Mr Warbucks will find your mother and father. I promise. If he has to put everyone in his organization on the job. If he has to pull every political string there is to pull. Up to and including the White House. Or even the League of Nations!'

'Gee whiz,' exclaimed Annie in a sudden change of mood, 'he's sure a powerful man.'

'He sure is,' said Miss Farrell with a smile.

Meanwhile, in his bedroom, having thought better of bringing Annie a brandy and having instead downed a shot of brandy himself, Mr Warbucks was already on the phone to Washington, to J. Edgar Hoover, the Director of the Federal Bureau of Investigation. 'J. Edgar, this is Warbucks speaking,' Mr Warbucks said with authority into the phone. 'For a special project of mine, to find the lost parents of a young New York girl, I want fifty of your best G-men . . . For a day, a week, months. For however long it will take to find them. Put them on vacation and I'll pay the costs. No matter how much . . . Fine. When can I have them? . . . Tomorrow

morning. Good. Oh, and J. Edgar, I want Special Agent
Gunderson . . . What? Well, just take him off the
Dillinger case!'

With that, Mr Warbucks hung up the phone on the
FBI Director and, once again in command of himself,
strode back to his study and stood towering over Annie.
'Annie,' he ordered, 'give me your locket.'

'But, Mr Warbucks,' Annie hesitated, 'I just told you
that . . .'

'I understand,' Mr Warbucks told her. 'But it could
be our best clue. We'll hand it over to the FBI and
they'll trace where it was bought. And then find out
who bought it.'

'Okay,' agreed Annie, reluctantly taking off the locket
and handing it to Mr Warbucks. She thought for a
moment and then reached into her pocket and took out
her note, which, like the locket, she had with her always.
'And maybe they should have my note, too,' added
Annie, handing the note to Mr Warbucks.

'Yes, a good idea, ' Mr Warbucks said. 'You watch,
Annie, I'm going to mount a coast-to-coast search for
your parents the likes of which has never been seen
before. If we have to, we'll check on every husband and
wife in America. And we'll find them. In fact, Annie,
you may be meeting your mother and father within a
couple of days.'

'Really?' asked Annie.

'Really,' said Mr Warbucks.

'Oh, boy!' cried Annie happily. 'I gotta go write a
letter to the kids at the orphanage about this!' And she
went dashing off to her bedroom. Mr Warbucks
motioned for Miss Farrell to go, and she, too, went from

the room, leaving him standing alone in his study. He picked up the adoption papers from his desk and flung them to the floor. Then he sat wearily down at his desk. 'Well, that's it,' he said to himself with a sigh. 'I'll find her mother and father for Annie and lose her for myself.' And, with that, Oliver Warbucks put his head down on his desk and wept.

TWELVE

Mr Warbucks was true to the promise he had made Annie. Putting aside all other business, he worked day and night directing a massive nationwide search for Annie's parents. By the following morning, he'd seen to it that headline stories about the search appeared on the front page of every newspaper in the United States. And, buying commercial time on radio stations all across the country, Mr Warbucks broadcast a recorded appeal to Annie's parents that was repeated every hour on the hour for days. Meanwhile, the FBI agents whom he'd borrowed from J. Edgar Hoover had joined in the search, along with over twenty thousand Warbucks factory workers who were excused from their jobs to make door-to-door canvasses in search of Annie's parents. Each day, over every major American city, skywriters in Warbucks-hired planes wrote the same message over and over again, 'Annie's parents, contact Oliver Warbucks.' Within forty-eight hours, in fact, there was scarcely anyone in the United States who hadn't heard about Annie and her dream of finding her lost parents.

In none of the stories that Mr Warbucks released about Annie, however, did he reveal the exact contents of her note or mention the fact that she'd been wearing a broken silver locket when she'd been left at the orphanage. 'That's information that only your real parents could have,' explained Mr Warbucks. 'So, if a couple comes forward knowing everything that was written in your note, like your date of birth, and also having the other half of your locket, then we'll know that they're really your mother and father.'

'I see,' said Annie. 'That way we can't be fooled by fakes who only claim to be my mother and father.'

'Exactly,' Mr Warbucks exclaimed.

On Tuesday evening, a few days before Christmas and five days after the nationwide search had begun, Annie and Mr Warbucks appeared as special guests on the most popular radio programme in America, an hour-long comedy-variety show called 'The Oxydent Hour of Smiles,' which starred a hammy comedian-singer named Bert Healy. Scheduled to go on towards the end of the programme, Annie and Mr Warbucks sat nervously on the stage of a huge midtown theatre before an audience of over a thousand while Bert Healy and his cast of regulars – a trio of blonde singers, the Boylan Sisters; a masked announcer named Jimmy Johnstone; and a ventriloquist named Fred McCracken and his dummy, Wacky – sang songs and did a series of comedy sketches that everyone but Annie and Mr Warbucks seemed to find hilarious. At last, Annie was summoned to the microphone by Bert Healy and asked to tell her story to the millions who were listening to the programme all over the United States.

'Thank you, Annie, thannnnk you, Annie,' Bert Healy crooned when she had finished speaking. 'On America's favourite radio programme, "The Oxydent Hour of Smiles", starring your old softy, Bert Healy, a moment of sadness.'

'Thank you, Bert Healy,' said Annie, tiptoeing back to her seat and sitting down next to Mr Warbucks.

'Good going, Annie,' whispered Mr Warbucks, squeezing her hand.

'But still,' Bert Healy went on, 'remembering my motto, folks . . .'

'Smile, darn ya, smile,' squeaked the ventriloquist's dummy, Wacky, in a high little voice.

'That's right, Wacky,' Healy said, 'smile, darn ya, smile. And now, from station WEAF in New York and over the coast-to-coast facilities of the NEB Red Network, it is my great pleasure to introduce to you none other than that very wealthy industrialist and Wall Street tycoon . . . Oliver Warbucks!'

The audience applauded enthusiastically as Mr Warbucks joined Bert Healy at the microphone. He nervously clutched a script that had been written for him by the show's writers.

'Good evening, Oliver Warbucks, it's nice of you to drop by,' said Healy.

'Good evening, Bert Healy, it is nice to be here,' read Mr Warbucks from his script.

'Oliver Warbucks,' said Healy, who was also reading from a script, 'I understand that you have some further details to tell the folks at home about wonderful little Annie here.'

'Yes, Bert Healy, I do,' Mr Warbucks enunciated carefully, 'Annie is a twelve-year-old foundling who was left by her parents on the steps of the New York City Municipal Orphanage, Girls' Annex, on St Mark's Place, on the night of December thirty-first, 1921.'

136

'And aren't you now conducting a coast-to-coast, nationwide search for Annie's parents?' asked Healy.

'Yes, Bert Healy,' replied Mr Warbucks, 'I am now conducting a coast-to-coast, nationwide search for Annie's parents. Furthermore, I'm announcing tonight for the first time that I am offering a certified cheque for fifty thousand dollars to any person who can prove they are Annie's parents.'

'Wow, that's great!' exclaimed Annie, jumping up from her chair and joining the audience in applauding Mr Warbucks.

'Fifty thousand dollars,' said Healy, 'wow, that's great.'

'Oh, boy – oh, boy – oh boy, fifty thousand smackers – I sure could use that kind of dough to help out my poor old mum,' joked Wacky, the dummy. 'She's a redwood tree in California.'

'Shh, quiet, Wacky, this is no joke,' warned Mr McCracken, the ventriloquist.

'I know, McCracken,' said Wacky. 'Everything you say is no joke. And you move your lips, too.'

'So, Annie's parents, if you're listenin' in,' Healy went on, 'write to Oliver Warbucks care of this station, WEAF, New York, or directly to him at . . .'

'At my home, Bert Healy,' furnished Mr Warbucks, 'nine eighty-seven Fifth Avenue, New York, New York.'

'That's nine eighty-seven Fifth Avenue, New York, New York,' said Healy. 'Thank you, Oliver Warbucks.'

Mr Warbucks was about to return to his seat when Healy suddenly shoved another page of script into his hands and motioned him to read it.

'Thank you, Bert Healy,' read Mr Warbucks from the

137

page he'd never seen before. 'And I would also like to take this opportunity to thank the makers of my favourite toothpaste, all-new Oxydent, with miracle K-64 to fight bad breath, for letting me appear here this evening. Good night, Bert Healy.' Mr Warbucks cast an angry glance at Healy for having duped him into delivering a toothpaste commercial and stomped back into his seat.

'Good night, Oliver Warbucks,' Healy said. 'And, Annie's parents, if you're out there, remember there's fifty thousand dollars and a wonderful daughter waiting for you.'

'So, get in touch right away, you hear,' Wacky ordered.

'Well, I see by the old clock on the wall that another of our Tuesday-evening get-togethers has gone by faster than you can say Oxydent.'

'O-x-y-d-e-n-t!' sang the Boylan Sisters in close harmony, off key.

'Yes, O-x-y-d-e-n-t, the toothpaste of the stars – the toothpaste of Frances Dee, Frances Farmer, and Kay Francis, to make your teeth Hollywood bright,' said Healy. 'So, for all of the "Hour of Smiles" gang – Ronnie, Bonnie, and Connie, the lovely Boylan Sisters; Fred McCracken . . .'

'And Wacky!' chimed in Wacky.

'And Jimmy Johnstone, radio's only masked announcer,' added Johnstone.

'This is your old softy, Mrs Healy's boy, Bert,' said Healy, 'saying until next week, same time same station, *bon soir, buenos noches, gute Nacht, buona sera,* and, gosh, I almost forgot, good night!'

All across the United States, tens of thousands of Americans had heard Mr Warbucks offer fifty thousand dollars to Annie's parents on Bert Healy's radio show. And among them had been Pepper, Duffy, Kate, Tessie, and Molly at the orphanage. Annie had written them that she was to be on the programme that night, and so they'd sneaked downstairs after lights-out to listen to 'The Hour of Smiles' in Miss Hannigan's office.

'Gee, Annie on the radio, from coast to coast – she's famous,' Kate exclaimed as the five orphans huddled wide-eyed around the radio, amazed to hear the voice of someone they actually knew coming into the room from far away.

'I wish I was on the radio,' Molly said wistfully.

'Me, too,' agreed Tessie.

'Nahhh, not me – who'd want to be on the dumb old radio,' said Pepper sourly, switching off Miss Hannigan's radio.

'Yeah, the dumb old radio,' muttered Duffy, who always agreed with everything that Pepper said.

Another person who'd heard 'The Oxydent Hour of Smiles' was Miss Hannigan herself, who'd listened to it from a barstool down the street at Sweeney's Shamrock Saloon. Now, toddling drunkenly home to the orphanage, she heard the orphans, talking and giggling in her office. She flung open the door and confronted them. 'Do I hear happiness in here?' shrieked Miss Hannigan.

The orphans quickly scurried into a line and stood at attention. 'No, Miss Hannigan,' they chorused.

'Whatta ya doin' up, down here?' Miss Hannigan demanded.

'Annie was on the radio,' said Molly.

'On WEAF,' added Kate.

'Yeah, I heard her, too,' said Miss Hannigan. 'Next thing you knows she'll be in the funny papers. Now, get outta here, get upstairs, get back to bed!'

'Yes, Miss Hannigan,' said the orphans, hurrying back upstairs to their beds before Miss Hannigan could get after them with her paddle.

In her bedroom behind the office, Miss Hannigan got into a grey flannel nightgown and poured herself a nightcap from the quart of Four Roses whiskey she kept on the table next to her bed. All the while she muttered to herself about the money that Oliver Warbucks had offered to Annie's parents. 'Fifty thousands bucks – what I couldn't do with fifty thousand bucks,' grumbled Miss Hannigan drunkenly. 'And me that raised the damn kid not gettin' a red cent. Oh, God, I hate that Annie so much you'd think I was her stepmother.'

Two others who'd listened to 'The Oxydent Hour of Smiles' that night were Rooster Hannigan and his lady friend, Lily St Regis, who heard the programme on the radio in their dingy room in the Hotel Dixie, on West 42nd Street near Times Square. 'Fifty thousand bucks – there's gotta be a way we can get our hands on that dough,' said Rooster, angrily pacing the floor of the small, airless hotel room. Suddenly, Rooster snapped his fingers and smiled a sinister, crooked smile: he'd had an idea. 'Listen, Lily,' he said, lowering his voice to a whisper, 'remember how we took that old lady in Atlantic City for three hundred bucks – made her think we was her long-lost brother and sister?'

'Sure, Rooster, that was the best bunco job we ever

pulled off,' Lily recalled.

'Yeah, up 'til now – but that's gonna be peanuts compared to this,' Rooster bragged. 'Lily, unpack that old dress you wear. We got ourselves a job to do.'

'You mean . . . ?' Lily asked.

'Yeah,' said Rooster, 'the return of America's sweetest and most lovable couple, Ralph and Shirley Mudge.'

An hour and a half later, Miss Hannigan was awakened from a drunken sleep by the ringing of the front doorbell. 'Who the hell can that be at this hour?' she mumbled to herself, putting on slippers, and her peach-coloured flannel bathrobe and going to the door. Standing meekly on the front steps was a tall, stooped man with grey hair, spectacles and droopy pepper-and-salt moustache. He was wearing black overshoes and a shabby brown overcoat, and he held his hat trembling in his hand. With him was a plump, grey-haired woman in a black lambskin coat that had seen better days. At their feet was a pair of battered suitcases tied shut with pieces of rope.

'Yeah, what is it?' Miss Hannigan demanded suspiciously as she stared at the woebegone couple.

'Excuse us, ma'am, but are you the lady that runs this here orphanage?' asked the man in a gentle, frightened voice.

'Yeah, that's me,' said Miss Hannigan as the man and woman stepped into the front hallway with their suitcases.

'Oh, sweetheart, I'm scared,' said the woman to the man. 'Somethin' coulda happened to her.'

141

'Hush, dear, it's gonna be all right,' the man assured her. 'She's gonna be here and she's gonna be our kid again.' He turned to Miss Hannigan. 'Ma'am,' he asked, 'was you workin' here twelve years ago?'

'Yeah,' Miss Hannigan curtly replied.

'Well, we had terrible money troubles back then – along towards the end of 1921,' the man said. 'And for a job that come up, we had to head north, to Canada.'

'A job on a farm – but they could only take the two of us,' the woman explained.

'So, you see, well, we had to leave our baby here,' said the man.

'Our little girl – our Annie,' crooned the woman, her eyes misting with tears.

'Annie?' asked Miss Hannigan, dumbfounded. 'You're Annie's parents?'

'Yes, ma'am, we are,' said the man.

'Please, ma'am, nothin's happened to her, has it?' the woman begged.

'I can't believe this,' said Miss Hannigan. 'After all these years. Annie's parents. Where'd you say you came from again?'

'We came from a little farm way up in Canada,' the woman replied.

'Yeah,' said the man, 'where they got plenty of chickens and ducks and geese and . . . *roosters*!' And with that, pulling off his moustache to show that it was fake, flapping his arms, and loudly crowing like a rooster, the man revealed himself to be none other than Rooster Hannigan in disguise. And with a high-pitched giggle, the woman whipped off her grey wig to reveal that she was none other than Lily St Regis.

142

'Ha, gotcha, Sis!' crowed Rooster, roaring with laughter.

'Oh, God, Rooster,' said Miss Hannigan, 'I never woulda knowed it was you in a hundred years.'

'Fooled ya, Aggie,' Rooster jeered. 'And, Lily, if we can fool my own sister, we can fool anybody. Including Warbucks.'

'Yeah, we're gona fool Warbucks outta fifty thousand smackers,' giggled Lily.

'Aggie, this is gonna be the best bunco job I ever pulled off,' Rooster said as the three of them went into Miss Hannigan's office and settled in chairs around her desk. 'I know a guy out in Brooklyn who can doctor up a fake birth certificate or any other kinda papers we want. But we need your help, Sis, for details. Details about Annie that can help us pull this thing off.'

'Sure, I could help you,' said Miss Hannigan. 'I could help you plenty. With little facts like Annie's date of birth, which was in that note of hers. But what's in it for me?'

'A three-way split, Aggie,' offered Rooster. 'One-third for you, one-third for me, and one-third for Lily.'

'Uh-uh, I want half or nothin' – twenty-five grand,' Miss Hannigan firmly stated.

'Half!' screeched Lily. 'That ain't fair – we'll be takin' a bigger risk than you.'

'Half or nothin',' repeated Miss Hannigan.

'Okay, damn it, half – twenty-five for you and twenty-five for the two of us,' said Rooster. 'And we're gonna do it fast, Aggie. I'll give 'em some of the old Rooster razzle-dazzle. Into Warbucks' joint on Fifth Avenue and out. Four, five minutes at the most. Get the money, get

Annie, and get the hell outta town.'

'Yeah, Annie. That's the problem.' Miss Hannigan hesitated. 'What are we gonna do with her afterwards?'

'Annie won't be no problem,' said Rooster, pulling out a switchblade knife and clicking it open. 'When I want somebody to disappear, they disappear. For good.' Rooster closed the knife and slipped it back into his jacket. 'And, like they say,' he added with an ugly, twisted grin, 'dead kids tell no tales.'

THIRTEEN

At seven o'clock on the grey, overcast morning of Wednesday, December 21st, Annie and Mr Warbucks boarded a special train at Pennsylvania Station and set off for Washington, DC, where Mr Warbucks was to meet with President Roosevelt at the White House. Settled in plush upholstered chairs in Mr Warbucks' private railroad car, which was furnished with Oriental rugs and expensive French antiques, Annie and Mr Warbucks talked about their appearance the night before on 'The Oxydent Hour of Smiles'. 'It sure was a dumb programme,' remarked Annie. 'Yes, but everyone except us seems to love it – probably half the country was listening in,' Mr Warbucks pointed out. 'And somewhere in America there's got to be someone who knows who your parents are.' The train went through a long tunnel and then passed for a time through a low-lying landscape of bleak, foul-smelling meadows. 'What's this place?' asked Annie, wrinkling up her nose as she pointed out the window at the dreary scene. 'New Jersey,' said Mr Warbucks, pulling down the window shade.

A few hours later, in the Oval Office of the White House, President Roosevelt and the members of his Cabinet sat bluntly listening to a news commentary on

145

the radio. '. . . . and has so far lived up to none of his lofty campaign promises – all we have had from Franklin D. Roosevelt and his so-called Brain Trust is a great deal of high-flown talk and virtually no action,' intoned the German-accented voice of America's most famous radio newscaster, H. V. Kaltenborn. 'In a nation racked by poverty, misery, and unemployment, it is deeds we want from the White House, not words. In short, Mr President, if you are listening, we've had enough of your fireside chats. It is time that you . . .'

President Roosevelt leaned over and clicked off the radio, cutting Kaltenborn off in mid-sentence. He placed a cigarette in his long silver cigarette holder, lighted it, and turned to the frowning members of his Cabinet.

'Criticism, damn it, nothing but criticism,' muttered Harold Ickes, the Secretary of the Interior.

'I know, I know,' Miss Frances Perkins, the Secretary of Labour, nodded in agreement.

'It's terrible,' grumbled Cordell Hull, the Secretary of State.

'Did you all read what they had to say about us in the Washington *Post* this morning?' dolefully asked Henry Morgenthau, Jr., the Acting Secretary of the Treasury.

'Please, don't bring that up,' groaned Louis Howe, the President's special economic aide and best friend.

President Roosevelt, who'd been confined to a wheelchair since 1921 (his legs were paralyzed by polio), turned the wheels of his chair to the Cabinet now and flashed his famous grin, 'My friends, I say again, the only thing we have to fear is fear itself!' the President cried cheerfully.

'Ah, baloney,' said Ickes, shaking his head as he and the others slumped deeper in gloom around the gleaming mahogany conference table.

'Every cloud has a silver lining?' suggested President Roosevelt. The members of the Cabinet sighed.

'In the words of radio's Bert Healy, "Smile, darn ya, smile," ' President Roosevelt said hopefully. The members of his Cabinet grimaced and looked gloomier than ever. A Marine guard entered the Oval Office with a gold-bordered calling card, which he handed to Louis Howe.

'Oliver Warbucks and friend, Mr President,' Howe read from the card.

'Friend?' questioned President Roosevelt. 'I don't know who his friend can be. But, in any case, show them in.'

'Yes, sir,' said the guard, and a moment later he ushered Mr Warbucks and Annie into the office.

'Ah, Oliver, how good of you to come,' smiled President Roosevelt, shaking Mr Warbucks' hand. Annie, who was wearing a blue-and-white organdie dress that Miss Farrell had specially bought for the trip to Washington, stood half hidden behind Mr Warbucks. She was awed to find herself in the presence of no less a man than the President of the United States. 'And, ah, who is this we have here?' asked the President, spying Annie.

'Mr President, this is my good friend Annie,' said Mr Warbucks. 'She so wanted to meet you that I couldn't resist bringing her along. Just to say hello.'

147

'Annie?' President Roosevelt was confused. But then he remembered. 'Ah,yes, of course – the little girl who spoke so beautifully on the radio last night.'

'Annie, this is President Roosevelt,' said Mr Warbucks.

'How do you do, Mr President Roosevelt?' murmured Annie, nervously shaking hands with the President.

'How do you do, Annie?' said President Roosevelt. 'You're as lovely as you sounded on the radio.'

'Thank you, Mr President Roosevelt,' Annie quietly answered.

'Well, shall we begin our meeting?' asked President Roosevelt, wheeling his wheelchair to the head of the conference table.

'Annie, if you'll wait outside,' whispered Mr Warbucks to Annie, 'I'll be out in . . .'

'No, no, Oliver, Annie can stay,' the President declared. 'Having a child on hand will keep us on our best behaviour.'

'Thank you, Mr President,' said Mr Warbucks. He and Annie found seats for themselves at the far end of the conference table.

'Now, goddamn it, wait a minute, this isn't a kindergarten for . . .' began Ickes, angrily frowning. A sixty-year-old curmudgeon, Ickes was well known for his short temper and his blunt use of four-letter words.

'Harold, while Annie is in the room I don't want to hear even so much as a "gosh" out of you,' commanded President Roosevelt with a smile. The President now introduced Annie to the Cabinet members, all of whom,

148

except Ickes, warmly shook her hand. And then the meeting began.

'Now, Oliver, since you speak for those happy few Americans who have any money left,' said President Roosevelt, 'I'd like to begin with your view on matters.'

'Mr President, in the words of that great Republican, Calvin Coolidge, "The business of this country is business," ' pronounced Mr Warbucks, rising to his feet. 'And for the good of you, the country, Wall Street, and *me*, we've got to get my factories open and the workers back to work.'

'I agree,' spoke up Miss Perkins, a doughty middle-aged spinster wearing a tricorn hat. She was the first woman ever to serve as a cabinet member. 'According to our latest figures at the Department of Labour, there are now fifteen million Americans out of work and nearly fifty million – a third of the population of this country – with no visible means of support or . . .'

'Mr President, if I may say so, unemployment is *not* our worst problem,' interrupted Cordell Hull. As Secretary of State, Hull was mainly concerned with foreign relations. 'The dispatches from Germany are becoming more and more disturbing each day,' Hull went on. 'There could be war.'

'Germany, hell!' growled Ickes. 'People are starving in this country.'

'Harold, I know that,' said Hull, 'but in the long run they . . .'

'Cordell,' broke in President Roosevelt, raising his hand for silence, 'for people who are starving there is no "long run".'

149

'The trouble is, everything is going wrong at once,' said Morgenthau unhappily. 'The stock market has taken another nose dive.'

'Sit-down strikes, riots, floods, dust storms,' grumbled Ickes.

'And the FBI still hasn't caught Public Enemy Number One, John Dillinger,' added Howe.

'Well, at least we're all agreed on one thing,' President Roosevelt said with a wry grin. 'The situation is hopeless and getting worse.'

At the far end of the table, Annie had sat quietly listening to all of this. But now, scarcely realizing what she was doing, she spoke up boldly. 'The sun'll come out tomorrow,' said Annie. 'Bet your bottom dollar that tomorrow there'll be sun!'

'Shush, quiet, little girl,' snapped Ickes.

'Harold!' reprimanded President Roosevelt, shaking his finger to silence Ickes. 'What did you say, Annie?'

Annie looked shyly around at Mr Warbucks and the others, surprised at herself and frightened that she'd spoken up in a White House Cabinet meeting. 'No, that's all right, Annie,' said President Roosevelt soothingly. 'Go ahead, my dear. It's still a free country, with free speech, where everyone gets to have his or her say.'

Annie took a deep breath and spoke up again. 'Well, I figure that if you can just think about the good things that might be comin' tomorrow instead of about the bad things that are happenin' today, you could sorta get started on makin' those good things come,' Annie said, and she went on to explain the simple optimistic philosophy that had got her through all of her years in the orphanage. As she spoke, President Roosevelt and the members of his Cabinet slowly began to smile, and the gloom that had pervaded the room miraculously began to lift. Suddenly, everyone, including Harold Ickes, was inspired with a new sense of hope. And, excitedly, they began jotting down ideas on the note pads in front of them on the conference table.

'Annie,' President Roosevelt declared when she'd finished speaking,'while listening to you I just decided that if my administration is going to be anything, it is going to be optimistic about the future of this country!'

'Well said – I agree!' cried Miss Perkins enthusiastically.

The Marine guard came into the office with a telegram for President Roosevelt. 'Excuse me, everyone,' murmured the President, opening the telegram and silently scanning it. 'Wait, this isn't for me,' said President, 'it's for you, Oliver, from your secretary in New York, "Hundreds of couples jamming street outside house, all claiming to be Annie's parents. Have begun to screen them. Suggest you return New York at once." Signed, Grace Farrell.'

'Well, I'll be darned,' Mr Warbucks said. 'It looks as though "The Oxydent Hour of Smiles" has even more listeners than we realized, huh, Annie?'

'Gee, hundreds of couples!' exclaimed Annie, leaping happily to her feet. 'One of them is bound to be my real mother and father!'

'We'll, Oliver, as much as I'm enjoying your company,' smiled President Roosevelt, 'and especially

151

yours, too, Annie, I suspect you'd better get back to New York immediately.'

'Yes, Mr President, if you don't mind,' said Mr Warbucks, taking Annie by the hand. 'Come along, Annie.'

'Bye, everybody,' Annie called.

'Bye, Annie,' answered the members of the Cabinet.

'Good-bye, Mr President, and thank you,' Annie said, awkwardly curtsying.

'No, thank *you*, Annie – you're the kind of person a president should have around him,' responded President Roosevelt, casting a sidelong glance at Ickes and the others. Annie gave President Roosevelt a kiss on the cheek and ran off, hand in hand with Mr Warbucks. Outside, by the East Gate, Annie and Mr Warbucks got into a limousine that – led by a siren-blaring escort of motorcycle policemen – sped to Union Station and the special train that was waiting to take them back to New York. Meanwhile, in the Oval Office, President Roosevelt and the members of his Cabinet were fired up with the new spirit of optimism that Annie had awakened in them.

'Mr President, what if we set up a hundred or even a thousand new federal projects,' Ickes cried excitedly, banging his fist on the conference table.

'Yes, like building new dams that would at the same time provide cheap electric power and create fertile new farmlands from thousands of acres that are now under water,' Morganthau suggested.

'We could build new highways, too,' said Miss Perkins.

'And post offices,' contributed Hull.

'And, of course, put the unemployed to work building them,' Ickes added.

'A wonderful idea,' said Miss Perkins. 'We could create five million new jobs within six months.'

'And weekly paychecks would get all of those millions off of federal assistance and back to paying taxes,' Morgenthau explained.

'We'll build a country so strong that nobody, including Chancellor Hitler, could ever defeat us in a war,' said Hull eagerly.

'The FBI caught Baby Face Nelson, didn't they?' asked How. 'They're bound to catch Dillinger.'

'Mr President,' urged Ickes, getting eagerly to his feet, 'what we've got to give this country is nothing less than a new . . . outlook.'

'A new . . . vision,' said Miss Perkins.

'A new . . . approach,' said Hull.

'A new . . . concept,' said Morgenthau.

'A new . . . dedication,' said Ickes.

'A new . . . horizon,' said Miss Perkins.

'A new . . . spirit,' said Hull.

'A new . . . attitude,' said Morgenthau.

"No, I know what we've got to give the American people,' cried President Roosevelt, as the Cabinet members grouped expectantly around him. 'We've got to give them . . . a New Deal!' The Cabinet members smiled and applauded – the President had hit on exactly the right phrase to describe what they wanted to do for America. 'Miss Perkins, gentlemen,' President Roosevelt went on, 'I was right the first time. The only thing we have to fear *is* fear itself!'

And so it was that, because of Annie, Franklin D.

Roosevelt's famed New Deal, which lifted the United States out of the worst depression in its history, was dreamed up in the White House one grey day in 1933. Or at least so says one legend of that long-ago year.

FOURTEEN

Earlier that morning, shortly after Annie and Mr Warbucks had left for Washington, a milling and shouting crowd of couples that eventually numbered more than a thousand people began to gather on Fifth Avenue in front of Mr Warbucks' mansion. Each of the couples claimed to be Annie's father and mother, and each loudly demanded to see Mr Warbucks. There were fat couples, thin couples, tall couples, short couples, old couples, and young couples, but they all had one thing in common – a burning desire to get their hands on Mr Warbucks' certified check for fifty thousand dollars.

When Drake opened the front door at eight o'clock to find the couples shouting for admission, he hurriedly locked the door again and raced upstairs to tell Miss Farrell what was going on. She at once took charge of the situation. 'Of course, they've all obviously got to be frauds – except one couple among them who might be Annie's parents,' reasoned Miss Farrell. 'And that's the couple we've got to single out.'

'If Annie's parents are out there, you'll find them, Miss Farrell,' Drake assured her.

'You're darned tootin' I will!' said Miss Farrell, using an expression she'd picked up from Mr Warbucks.

Miss Farrell set up a plan of action. She typed and had a thousand copies made of a questionnaire she'd quickly drawn up. The questionnaire consisted of ten questions, requiring such routine information as name, address, and age, but it ended with a crucial tenth question: 'On the night that Annie was left at the orphanage, something was left with her. What was it?' Next, Miss Farrell had Drake and a platoon of other servants pass out the questionnaires to the horde of couples, who were now being confined to the sidewalks on either side of Fifth Avenue by a squad of policemen mounted on chestnut horses. The couples were told to fill out the questionnaires, form a line, and wait for their turn to be interviewed inside the Warbucks mansion by Miss Farrell. In the foyer, Miss Farrell sat in a Chippendale chair behind a cherry-wood desk and saw all the couples in turn as they were led in, two by two, like the animals filing on to Noah's ark.

It was a simple matter for Miss Farrell to dismiss almost all of the couples all but instantly, for they had incorrectly answered question ten, guessing wrongly that Annie had been left at the orphanage with everything from a grilled cheese sandwich to a Shetland pony. Occasionally, Miss Farrell came upon a couple who – by luck, as matters turned out – guessed that Annie had been left with a locket. But, upon closer questioning, none of them had come up with the vital information that it had been half of a broken silver locket.

Hour after hour, stopping only briefly to have a tuna-fish sandwich and a cup of hot Ovaltine at her desk, Miss Farrell carefully screened one fraudulent couple after another. As each new couple stepped up to her desk, she silently prayed that they might be Annie's

156

parents, but her prayers went unanswered. And by five o'clock, as dusk was coming down over the grey city, she'd seen the last of the false parents. There were no more couples waiting outside. Now, exhausted, Miss Farrell put her head down on the desk and quietly wept.

Drake looked outside once more and then locked the huge, carved-oak front door. 'I'm afraid, Miss Farrell, that was the last of them,' he said. 'And there's still no sign of Mr Warbucks and Miss Annie.'

Miss Farrell dried her tears with a blue silk handkerchief. 'Drake, look at all the questionnaires,' she sighed, pointing to the enormous stack of papers piled on the desk in front of her. 'Do you realize that I talked to six hundred and twenty-seven women who claimed to be Annie's mother and six hundred and nineteen men who said that they were her father? That makes, let me see . . .'

'One thousand two hundred and forty-six, miss,' furnished Drake instantly.

'All liars, said Miss Farrell with a weary shake of her head. 'Drake, I never realized that there were so many dishonest people on the island of Manhattan.'

'Some of them were from the Bronx, miss,' observed Drake dryly.

A key turned in the front door and Annie and Mr Warbucks came bursting in. 'Grace, we're back!' cried Mr Warbucks.

'Where are they, Miss Farrell?' asked Annie breathlessly, her eyes aglow with hope as she rushed up to the secretary. 'Where are all the people who say they're my folks?'

'They're gone, dear,' said Miss Farrell, getting up

from the desk and coming around to pull Annie into her arms. She tried not to start weeping again. 'Come and gone. I'm sorry, Annie, but they were all liars and fakes, after nothing but the fifty thousand dollars.'

'Aw, gee,' said Annie, downhearted. For a moment, tears seemed to brim in her eyes, but she didn't cry.

'Are you certain, Grace?' Mr Warbucks demanded. The front doorbell rang, and Drake went to answer it.

'Yes, sir,' Miss Farrell answered. 'None of them knew about the locket. I'm so sorry.'

'Gosh,' said Annie. 'I was sure somebody was gonna be my mother and father.'

Drake returned from the front door with the trace of a smile on his usually stony face. 'Mr Warbucks, this has just come by special messenger from the FBI,' he said. He handed a large manila envelope to Mr Warbucks.

'Ah, at last!' cried Mr Warbucks, opening the envelope and taking out a letter that he quickly scanned. 'Good news! Agent Gunderson has located the manufacturer of Annie's locket. In Utica, New York.'

'Oh, boy!' shouted Annie.

'That sort of locket was manufactured between 1918 and 1924,' read Mr Warbucks.

'Sort of locket?' asked Miss Farrell, puzzled.

'Yes,' said Mr Warbucks, heaving a deep sigh as he read further in the letter. 'Over ninety thousand were manufactured and sold.'

'Aw, gee,' said Annie.

Mr Warbucks read through the rest of the letter with increasing disappointment. 'Annie,' he said at last, 'I'm afraid that the gist of it is that Agent Gunderson doesn't think that there's a chance in a million of tracing your parents through the locket. I'm sorry.' Mr Warbucks reached into the envelope and took out Annie's locket, returned by the FBI, and gently put it on her.

'That's okay, Mr Warbucks,' said Annie, touching her locket. She walked to the window and stood looking forlornly out on Fifth Avenue. 'I mean, gee,' she went on, 'you did the best you could. And if you can't find my folks, nobody can. Anyway, I guess a kid can get along without a mum and a dad. You did, from the time you was ten, and, heck, you didn't turn out all that bad.'

'Thank you, Annie,' Mr Warbucks said with a soft smile.

Sensing that Mr Warbucks wanted to be alone with Annie, Miss Farrell murmured, 'Excuse me, Mr Warbucks, we'll go check on the dinner menu,' and she took Drake by the arm and went off to the kitchen. Mr Warbucks went to Annie at the window and put his hand on her shoulder. 'Annie, you know, I've made me the greatest fortune in the world,' he said in an uncharacteristically gentle voice. 'I've owned mansions and yachts all over the world. I've had two universities named after me, I've been on the cover of *Time* magazine four times, and I'm told that I'm one of the five most famous and powerful men in the world. But yet, always, I've had a secret feeling that something was missing in my life. Something vastly important. And now, in these last days, I've finally found out what that something is.'

'What?' asked Annie, turning to him.

'You,' replied Mr Warbucks quietly. 'You're what's been missing in my life. Someone to care for.'

'Me?' asked Annie, a trifle bewildered.

159

'Yes, you,' said Mr Warbucks. Then, as if to break the mood, he loudly laughed and tousled Annie's red hair. He strode to the archway and called for Miss Farrell. In a moment, she came running in. 'Yes, sir?' she asked.

'Do you have those legal papers I gave you to file the other day?' asked Mr Warbucks.

'Oh, yes, sir!' cried Miss Farrell happily, realizing that he meant Annie's adoption papers. 'I'll get them right away!'

'No, wait, Grace, I want you to stay for a moment,' said Mr Warbucks, sitting down in the Chippendale chair and motioning for Annie to come to him. Annie sat on Mr Warbucks' knee, and he put his arm tightly around her. Now, as he spoke, he tried to sound as businesslike and unemotional as possible. 'Annie,' he said flatly, 'I want to adopt you.'

'*Adopt me?*' Annie could scarcely believe what she'd heard.

'Yes or no?' Mr Warbucks asked straightforwardly.

Annie was dazed. For a moment – as Mr Warbucks and Miss Farrell nervously waited to hear what she was going to say – Annie couldn't speak. 'Gee, if I can't have any real mother and father,' said Annie at last with a happy grin, 'then there's nobody in the world I'd rather have for a father than you, Mr Warbucks!' She flung her arms about his neck and hugged him. And he hugged her back. Miss Farrell started to step forward to hug both of them, but then she realized that this was their moment, not hers, and stepped back to look at the two of them with tears of joy in her eyes.

'Grace,' said Mr Warbucks happily, 'call Justice Brandeis and ask him to come over here on Saturday

160

night, Christmas Eve, to sign the adoption papers.'

'Yes, sir!' said Miss Farrell.

'And tell Mrs Pugh that we'll be having a houseful of guests on Saturday night,' Mr Warbucks went on. 'We'll need flowers, music, caviar, champagne!'

'Yes, sir, I'll go tell her right now!' cried Miss Farrell, running off to the kitchen.

Mr Warbucks stood up and took Annie exuberantly into his arms. 'Annie, this isn't just going to be an adoption, it's going to be a celebration!' he joyously shouted, whirling her about. 'And you can have anyone in the world you want to come to it. Who would you like? John D. Rockefeller? Clark Gable? Harpo Marx? Babe Ruth?'

'Anyone in the world?' pondered Annie as Mr Warbucks put her down gently. 'Well, I guess I'd like Miss Farrell, of course. And Mr Drake. And Mrs Pugh. And, well, I guess, I'd like everybody in the mansion here.'

'Of course, that's who I'd like, too,' smiled Mr Warbucks.

'Oh, and I'd like all of the kids from the orphanage, too,' Annie added.

'Oh, no, I'm afraid that it'll be a late party – way past their bedtime,' said Mr Warbucks. 'But, I'll tell you what, we'll have everyone from the orphanage here on Sunday morning, Christmas, for the biggest and best Christmas party that any kids have ever had!'

'Oh, boy!' cried Annie, but then she suddenly remembered who 'everyone at the orphanage' happened to include. 'But . . . Miss Hannigan, too?'

'Yes, of course, Miss Hannigan, too!' Mr Warbucks

said expansively. 'Why not? We'll forgive and forget!'

'Well . . . okay,' Annie reluctantly agreed.

'Annie' cried Mr Warbucks, once again sweeping her up in his arms, 'I'm the luckiest man in the world!'

'And I'm the luckiest kid!'

FIFTEEN

It was Christmas Eve at 987 Fifth Avenue, and in the middle of the living room of Oliver Warbucks' mansion stood a Christmas tree more beautiful than and nearly as big as the one in Rockefeller Center. And spread beneath the tree were more gifts than any child had ever dreamed of getting – there were dolls, dollhouses, bicycles, tricycles, hobbyhorses, life-size stuffed animals, games, books, puzzles, and electric-train sets, among scores of other toys. It looked as though Mr Warbucks had bought out the entire stock of the F. A. O. Schwartz toy store. A thirty-piece band led by Paul Whiteman was playing 'Jingle Bells' in the adjoining ballroom as servants moved through the crowd carrying trays of caviar and glasses abrim with French champagne. These were specially hired servants, for the regular servants of the house were, of course, the guests at tonight's very special party. Next to the holly-festooned fireplace, Miss Farrell, in a pale-lavender chiffon gown, was chatting with Justice Louis Brandeis, of the United States Supreme Court, who was wearing his black judicial robes.

The clock struck eight o'clock and all applauded as Mr Warbucks came smilingly down the marble staircase into the living room. He was elegantly got up in a Savile Row tuxedo with a glittering diamond stud in his shirt front that was only slightly larger and more expensive than the Hope diamond. Mr Warbucks signalled for the band to stop playing and addressed his assembled guests. He was about to refer to them as 'ladies and gentlemen of my staff', but then he thought better of it. He was no longer the cold employer of a faceless staff of servants he'd been until the time that Annie came into his life. Like the Tin Woodman in *The Wizard of Oz*, Oliver Warbucks had, late in life, got a heart. And so instead he now addressed his servants as 'my friends'. 'My friends, my dear friends, welcome to my lovely living room,' cried Mr Warbucks exultantly, 'and welcome, too, to the happiest night of my life!'

Everyone applauded, and the band began playing 'Joy to the World' as the crowd laughed and ate and drank while awaiting the arrival of the party's guest of honour. Upstairs, for hours, Annette and Cécille had been fussing over Annie. First, they'd given her a long, leisurely, perfumed bubble bath in a huge sunken bathtub. Then they'd given her a new hairdo, using a curling iron to curl her hair on top of her head, French style, in little red ringlets. And, finally, they'd dressed her in white silk stockings, black patent-leather Mary Jane shoes, and a new dress that Miss Farrell had bought her especially for tonight's party. The dress was red velvet, with white velvet trim at the V neck and waist. It was the most beautiful dress that Annie had ever seen,and she had loved it at first sight. 'I'll wear it forever!' Annie had exclaimed when Miss Farrell took it out of the Bergdorf Goodman box and showed it to her. When Annette and Cécille had finished, Annie looked at herself in the mirror – with her new hairdo and in the red dress, she scarcely recognized herself. 'Wow!' breathed Annie.

Now, Annie stood at the top of the staircase that led to the living room. Her heart was wildly beating with excitement and joy – she was about to become Oliver Warbucks' daughter! As she started down the staircase, everyone noticed her and began applauding. Annie grinned from ear to ear. When she reached the bottom of the stairs, Mr Warbucks rushed to her and picked her up in his arms. 'Annie, you look absolutely beautiful!' he cried. And then, as he hugged her close to him, he whispered to her, 'Together at last, together forever – I don't need anyone but you.' 'And I don't need anyone but you,' she whispered back to him, kissing him tenderly on the cheek.

Justice Brandeis cleared his throat and called for silence as he stepped forward with the adoption papers. 'Let us get this little bit of legal business out of the way, and then it'll be on with the party,' said the Justice. Everyone gathered around in a large circle as Annie and Mr Warbucks, hand in hand, stood before Justice Brandeis, looking almost like a couple about to be married. 'Now,' said Justice Brandeis, 'the adoption procedure is very simple . . .'

A strange sense of menace and cold fell suddenly over the room. A tall, shabbily dressed grey-haired man and a plump little grey-haired woman had been ushered into the room by one of the servants. 'Pardon us, folks, sorry to bust in on your party like this,' said the man in a cracking, elderly-sounding voice. 'Yeah, sorry,' croaked the woman. They were, of course, Rooster Hannigan and his girl friend, Lily St Regis, in disguise. After days of careful preparation Rooster was now carrying out his nefarious plan. He was going to swindle Oliver Warbucks out of fifty thousand dollars, abduct Annie, and do away with her.

'Oh, Shirley, look,' said Rooster, pointing at Annie, 'there's our Annie.'

'Who are you?' Annie asked. She didn't know who these people were, but she sensed immediately that there was something evil and dangerous about them.

'Honey, we're your mum and dad,' said Lily, her voice disguised as that of a middle-age woman.

'Mudge. Mudge is the name,' said Rooster, shuffling meekly across the room to Mr Warbucks. The guests and Justice Brandeis backed away. 'Ralph Mudge. And this here is the wife, Shirley.'

'You never knew it 'til now, honey, but you're Annie Mudge,' crooned Lily, taking Annie's hand. Her touch felt cold and clammy to Annie.

'Annie Mudge?' asked Annie.

'Annie Mudge?' repeated Mr Warbucks.

'Yup,' said Rooster. 'You see, honey, we was sick and broke back in 1921, and we didn't know which way to turn. But then a man gave us a chance to work on his farm up in Canada.' Rooster's story had been rehearsed for days.

'But we couldn't bring along no baby,' added Lily, delivering her prerehearsed line right on cue.

'We loved you, Annie, but we had to leave you behind,' said Rooster, pretending to wipe tears from his eyes.

Miss Farrell, who had of course already dealt with hundreds of frauds claiming to be Annie's parents, stepped between Mr Warbucks and Rooster. 'Mr Mudge, is it?' she asked, suspicious, certain that this couple were yet another pair of frauds. 'We have seen a great number of people who have claimed to be . . .'

'Ah, yes, proof,' said Rooster, reaching into his pocket and pulling out the false documents that his crony in Brooklyn had prepared. 'I expect you'll be wantin' proof of who we are. Here's our driver's licences and Annie's birth certificate.'

Miss Farrell took the papers and carefully examined them. 'Baby girl, named Anne Elizabeth Mudge,' she read aloud from the birth certificate, 'born to Ralph and Shirley Mudge, New York, New York, October twenty-eighth, 1921.'

'October twenty-eighth – that's my birthday!' cried Annie.

'It is, sir, it was in her note,' murmured Miss Farrell to Mr Warbucks.

'Yes, I know,' said Mr Warbucks, grave-faced and concerned. If they were frauds, October twenty-eighth could have been a lucky guess, thought Mr Warbucks, and yet that didn't seem probable. Only he, Annie, Miss Farrell, and the FBI knew Annie's date of birth. He didn't realize that one other person, Miss Hannigan, also knew it. And it was Miss Hannigan, of course, who had told it to Rooster. 'In any case,' Mr Warbucks went on, 'even if the date of birth is correct, I still don't . . .'

'Please, mister, you gotta believe us,' pleaded Rooster, blinking his eyes to summon up phony tears. 'We got in on the Greyhound bus this afternoon, and went straight to the orphanage to fetch our Annie. And the lady there, she said our baby was up here.'

Lily grabbed Annie and hugged her. 'Oh, Annie, all the years I dreamed of holdin' ya in my arms again,' she cooed. Annie wriggled out of Lily's embrace and ran to Mr Warbucks. Somehow she instinctively knew that this woman wasn't her mother.

Question ten, thought Grace, and she once again confronted Rooster. 'Mr Mudge,' she began. 'on the night that Annie was left at the orphanage, something was . . .'

'Oh, here's something none of you would know anything about,' said Rooster, reaching into his pocket and taking out half of a broken silver locket that he'd had a jeweller on Staten Island fix up for him. 'We left half of a silver locket with Annie, and kept this here other half so's we'd know when we come back for her that . . .'

'Oh, Ralph, look!' cried Lily. 'Annie's still wearin' it – my old locket from Grandma!'

'Let's see if the part we kept fits together with it,' said Rooster, stepping up to Annie and forcing the two pieces of the locket together. They fit, more or less – the jeweller had gone a good job from a description of Annie's half of the locket that Miss Hannigan had provided. 'Yes, they fit perfectly!' cried Rooster.

'Oh, thank God, Ralph – this proves that she's our Annie, all right,' breathed Lily.

Although they didn't want to believe it, Mr Warbucks and Miss Farrell were now unhappily convinced that Ralph and Shirley Mudge were indeed Annie's parents. 'Yes, she seems to be your Annie,' said Mr Warbucks quietly.

'Yes, she does,' Miss Farrell said sadly.

'Thank the good Lord we was able to prove to you

168

that Annie is our kid,' said Rooster. 'So, if you'll get Annie's things together, we'll be takin' her along – right now.' But we won't be taking her far, thought Rooster with an evil shudder, no farther than Sheepshead Bay, where we'll dump her body. He took Annie firmly by the arm and started to edge with Lily towards the front door.

'Take her? Now?' cried Mr Warbucks.

'Of course,' said Rooster. 'Why not? She's our kid.'

'But, Mr Mudge, what about the money?' Mr Warbucks asked.

This was the question that Rooster had been waiting for. Now, he'd hook Warbucks for certain. 'Money? Well, we ain't got much money, but we'd be glad to give you whatever we got for takin' care of our Annie,' said Rooster, reaching into his jacket as though to take out a wallet.

'You haven't heard that I've offered a certified cheque for fifty thousand dollars to any couple who can prove that they are Annie's parents?' Mr Warbucks demanded, taking the cheque from his pocket. He'd planned to donate it tonight to the March of Dimes as part of the celebration of Annie's adoption.

'No, sir,' lied Rooster smoothly. 'We don't know nothin' about no cheque. Anyway, we don't want no money.'

'Right,' Lily chimed in, 'we don't want no money for our Annie.'

Mr Warbucks and Miss Farrell exchanged glances of disbelief. If Ralph and Shirley Mudge didn't even want the fifty thousand dollars, then they were without doubt Annie's parents. Mr Warbucks slowly began to put the cheque back in his pocket.

'On the other hand, Shirley,' said Rooster quickly, not wanting to let his fish, Oliver Warbucks, get off the hook, 'maybe we could use a little money. For Annie's sake. Remember that little pig farm out in New Jersey, darling? With fifty thousand dollars, we could afford to bring Annie up right. In the country. With fresh air, fresh eggs . . .'

'Fresh ham,' said Lily pointedly to Rooster. She was afraid that he'd begun to play his part a little too broadly.

'Ah, yes, ha ha, ham,' chuckled Rooster, sidling up to Mr Warbucks and deftly flicking the cheque from his fingers. 'Certified, huh?' he asked, examining the cheque. 'All I gotta do is make this here cheque out to myself, huh?' Rooster started to put it in his pocket.

'Yes, that's correct,' said Mr Warbucks, taking the cheque back from Rooster and putting it in his own pocket, 'tomorrow morning.'

'Tomorrow morning?' asked Lily, aghast at what she'd just seen happen. Rooster had had the cheque and now he didn't.

'Yes,' said Mr Warbucks, 'I'm sure that you wouldn't mind if Annie stayed here until tomorrow morning, Christmas. Then you can come back to pick up Annie *and* the cheque.'

'Oh,' said Lily.

Rooster didn't know what to do. But he knew that he mustn't appear too eager to get his hands on the cheque if he was to get away with his scheme. If he'd have to wait until tomorrow to get the cheque, then he'd have to – at least he'd successfully conned Warbucks into believing that he and Lily were Annie's parents. 'Oh, well, yes – whatever you prefer, sir,' Rooster stammered. 'So, Shirley, I think we oughta be gettin' back to our hotel now. Bye, Annie.'

'Yes, bye, Annie, love,' crooned Lily sweetly. Once they got outside, she was going to break Rooster's neck for letting that cheque slip through his fingers.

'Until tomorrow morning, honey,' said Rooster, backing away from Annie and Mr Warbucks in the direction of Miss Farrell, who was standing behind him. 'And then you'll be spending the rest of your life with us.' Your very short life, thought Rooster evilly. 'Well, good-bye, all!' As he backed up, Rooster bumped roughly into Miss Farrell, all but knocking her off her feet. 'Oops, pardon me blondie,' he blurted, off guard, for a moment speaking not in the disguised voice of Ralph Mudge but instead in his normal voice. And, by chance, he'd uttered the exact words he'd said to Miss Farrell when he'd bumped into her at the orphanage. 'Merry Christmas!' cried Rooster, and he headed towards the front door. 'Yeah, Season's Greetin's, said Lily, following him out of the mansion.

Puzzled, remembering that someone, somewhere, had said those same words to her – 'Oops, pardon me, blondie' – in that same voice, Miss Farrell stared perplexedly at the departing Mudges. But who had said that to her? And where? And when?

After Mr and Mrs Mudge had gone, an awkward silence fell over the room. Annie stood alone beside the Christmas tree, staring down at the floor. Mr and Mrs Mudge were her father and mother. But they couldn't be. She'd have known her real mother and father the

instant they walked in the door. They just couldn't be.
Everyone at the party stood silently, uncertainly, not
knowing what to say.

'Well, this is . . . wonderful news, Annie,' said Mr
Warbucks, trying to sound cheerful.

'Yes . . . wonderful news,' muttered everyone.

'Annie has found her parents,' said Mr Warbucks
'and they seem to be a . . . a very nice couple.'

'Yes, very nice,' everyone murmured.

'You're lucky, Annie,' said Miss Farrell gently.

'Right, I'm lucky,' gulped Annie, trying not to cry
'Just think . . . New Jersey.'

'We have something even better than an adoption to
celebrate – so, please, champagne for everyone!' cried
Mr Warbucks, and glasses of champagne were quickly
passed around. 'We must have a wonderful evening,
Mr Warbucks went on, raising his champagne glass
'Because it is Christmas Eve and we have just had the
most wonderful news in the world. Annie has found her
mother and father. Everyone, I propose a toast. To
Annie Mudge!'

'To Annie Mudge!' all the guests repeated, raising
their glasses and glumly drinking. Annie could hold in
her unhappiness no longer. She burst into tears and ran
sobbing up the stairs to her bedroom.

'Annie, oh, Annie!' cried Miss Farrell, running to the
bottom of the stairs. She'd have gone up to comfor
Annie if it hadn't been for the arrival of another guest a
the party. Into the room, pushed by a Secret Service
man, came President Roosevelt in his wheelchair. Mr
Warbucks had forgotten that this was the night he'd
invited the President for supper.

'Merry Christmas!' called out President Roosevelt in his cheeriest voice. He was grinning broadly.

'Merry Christmas,' muttered everyone gloomily.

President Roosevelt swivelled around to look up at the Secret Service man behind him. 'I seem to have the same effect on everyone,' he said with a sigh.

Mr Warbucks stood alone by the fireplace. 'I've lost her,' he said quietly to himself. 'I've lost Annie.' Miss Farrell hurried up to him. 'Sir,' she said, 'that Mr Mudge, I think I've seen him somewhere before. I just can't remember where or when. But I have the strangest feeling that he's not who he says he is.'

If the Mudges were frauds, thought Mr Warbucks, then there was a chance that he hadn't lost Annie, after all. He had to find out for certain by tomorrow morning. But how? He'd never asked for any man's help, reflected Mr Warbucks, and he'd promised himself that he never would. But now he had to. Because, he suddenly understood, he wasn't as all-powerful as he'd always thought he was – he was as vulnerable as any other man in this world. And so Oliver Warbucks turned humbly now to President Roosevelt. 'Mr President, er, Franklin,' he said quietly, 'I need your help.'

'Of course, Oliver,' said President Roosevelt with great kindness. 'Whatever I can do for you, I'll do.'

SIXTEEN

All night long, Annie lay awake in her canopy bed. This is the last night I'll spend in this house, she thought sadly, staring up at the ceiling. From time to time, she dozed fitfully for a minute or two, drifting into happy dreams in which she and Mr Warbucks were sailing to Europe on a blue ocean liner or were riding together on a roller coaster at a seaside amusement park. But then she abruptly woke up to remember that she wasn't going to be Mr Warbucks' daughter, after all, and that in the morning she'd be on her way to New Jersey with Mr and Mrs Mudge. Her father and mother. 'For gosh sakes,' Annie said to herself, 'stop feelin' so darned sorry for yourself. The pig farm in New Jersey will probably be even nicer than right here. And once I get to know them, I'll bet that Mr and Mrs Mudge turn out to be real wonderful folks. Think of all that good fresh air. And pigs. Anyway, the sun'll come out tomorrow, bet your bottom dollar.'

Shortly before dawn, a light snow began to fall on New York, and Annie got up to stand at the window and watch the snow swirling down Fifth Avenue in the light of street lamps. She gazed forlornly at the falling snow just as she had from the window at the orphanage in the early hours of the beginning of 1933. But now her father and mother were actually soon coming for her. How strange that this thought, of all thoughts, should make her so unhappy. At last, a grey dawn arrived, and Annie put on her red dress and packed the Vuitton suitcase that Mr Warbucks had bought for her. Then she put on the pale-pink wool coat and hat from Best's, picked up her suitcase, and trudged downstairs to the living room. She sat on her suitcase next to the darkened Christmas tree and waited alone in the vast, shadowy room for Mr and Mrs Mudge to come for her. She looked around at all of the gifts under the tree. I guess I won't be getting any of them, she thought. Or maybe just one doll to take along to New Jersey.

The lights went on in the living room, and Annie turned to see Mr Warbucks and Miss Farrell standing in the archway, still dressed as they had been the night before for the party.

'Merry Christmas, Annie,' said Mr Warbucks.

'Merry Christmas, Annie,' said Miss Farrell.

'Merry Christmas, Mr Warbucks, Miss Farrell,' chirped Annie brightly, trying to smile and sound cheerful.

'You're up early, Annie,' said Mr Warbucks.

'Yes, sir,' replied Annie. 'Because, you see, my folks are comin' for me, of course, so I thought I'd just wait for 'em here. I guess they'll be takin' me out to the country.' She looked pleadingly up at Mr Warbucks. 'Will you come and see me sometime?' she asked.

'Yes, I'll see you, Annie,' said Mr Warbucks solemnly.

'You're up early, too,' said Annie.

'We've been up all night, dear,' said Mr Warbucks. 'And, we've had a quite a night of it. FBI men coming and going. I've been on the phone more than a dozen times with Mr Hoover, the Director of the FBI. And I've had a great deal of help from President Roosevelt. Annie, did you know that he's here?'

'President Roosevelt? Really?' asked Annie, popping excitedly up from her suitcase.

'Really,' said Mr Warbucks. 'Annie, I've got something very difficult to tell you, and the President is going to help me tell it to you.' Mr Warbucks stepped over to the archway and called 'Mr President, could you come in now, please?' and President Roosevelt appeared now in his wheelchair.

'Merry Christmas, Mr President Roosevelt,' said Annie.

'Merry Christmas, Annie,' said the President. 'It's good to see you again.'

'It's good to see you, too, sir,' said Annie.

Both Mr Warbucks and Miss Farrell looked anguished, and for once Mr Warbucks seemed unable to speak. 'Franklin, could you please tell her for me?' he asked the President in a hoarse whisper.

'Annie,' said the President, beckoning to her to come close to him and clasping her hand, 'early this morning, FBI Director Hoover telephoned us with some very sad news. Through the paper that your note was written on, his men succeeded late last night in tracing the identity of your parents.'

'Yes, we already know that,' Annie said. 'Mr and Mrs Mudge.'

'No, dear, they are't your parents,' said Mr Warbucks. 'Your parents were David and Margaret Bennett.'

'David and Margaret Bennett!' cried Annie. 'Where are they?'

'Annie . . .' began Mr Warbucks, but he was unable to continue.

'Annie,' said President Roosevelt quietly, 'your mother and father passed away. A long time ago. In January of 1922.'

'You mean . . . they're dead?' Annie asked.

'Yes, dear, they're dead,' said Mr Warbucks.

'So, I'm an orphan, after all, like the other kids.' Annie said. Brokenhearted, fighting back tears, Annie walked to the window and stood silently staring out on the falling snow. Her dream of finding her father and mother would never come true. Her parents were gone.

Agent Gunderson of the FBI had observed that Annie's note was written on a special kind of heavyweight drawing paper that was used mainly by artists. And after days of investigation, he'd discovered that that particular kind of paper was sold in New York at an artists' supply store only three blocks from the orphanage where Annie had been left. Rudolph T. Termohlen, the longtime proprietor of the store, had remembered that, years ago, a young painter named David Bennett had bought a large quantity of that type of paper from him. And, digging into his old sales records, Termohlen had found Bennett's address – 329 East Seventh Street. The address turned out to be that of a boardinghouse run by an aged Irish widow named Rose Riley. Mrs Riley remembered Mr Bennett and his young wife very well indeed. 'So sad, so very, very sad,' she told Agent Gunderson when he came to her door. 'Both of them so young, and to die of the influenza in that terrible, terrible epidemic of 1922.' Yes, Mrs Riley recalled, the Bennetts had had a baby daughter. But not long before they passed away, soon after Mrs Bennett had fallen ill, the baby had suddenly no longer been with them. 'I figured they sent her to live with grandparents or somebody,' explained Mrs Riley. She remembered that there was a boxful of the Bennetts' unclaimed belongings stored down in her cellar. In the box, Agent Gunderson found a photograph album, Margaret Bennett's diary, and, among other documents, Annie's birth certificate. From the diary, Agent Gunderson had pieced together the Bennetts' story. They'd come to New York from Iowa in early 1921 so that they could study art at Cooper Union. They were young – he was twenty-five and she was twenty-three. Impoverished, struggling artists who were alone in the world, with no families back in Iowa. So, when Margaret Bennett had become ill, her husband, desperately afraid that their baby might also catch influenza, had left Annie at the orphanage, intending to bring her back home as soon as his wife was well. But Margaret Bennett had died on January 13, 1922, and two weeks later, having caught the disease from his wife, David Bennett had also died. And he'd apparently become delirious with fever before he'd had a chance to tell anyone about Annie. The Bennetts were bright and talented artists, and from snapshots in the photograph album, Agent Gunderson could see that they'd been a handsome couple – he was tall and square-jawed, with a mop of unruly red hair, and she was a pretty, sweet-faced blonde. And, as a number of entries in Margaret Bennett's diary showed, she and her husband had loved Annie very much. Thus, the mystery was sadly solved of why Annie's parents had never come back for her.

For a long time, Annie stood silently at the window while Mr Warbucks, Miss Farrell, and President Roosevelt just as silently watched her. 'Are you all right, Annie?' Miss Farrell asked at last gently.

Annie turned to them. 'Yes,' she said. 'Because, you see, I guess I always knew, deep down, that my folks were dead. Because I knew they loved me. And so they would have come for me if . . if they weren't dead.' While standing at the window, Annie had made up her mind that she wasn't going to dwell on the sorrow of the past. Not even for a day. From this moment on, she told herself, I'm going to forget all that's gone by and just try to live my life as happily as I can.

Mr Warbucks walked towards Annie, stopped, and then held out his arms to her. Tears glistened in his eyes. 'I love you, Annie Bennett,' he said. Annie ran to him and threw herself into his arms. 'And I love you, too.' For a moment, they stood with their arms about each other in the middle of the room, and then Annie, as tough-spirited as ever, stepped back and loudly demanded to know, 'Now, who the heck are Ralph and Shirley Mudge?'

Mr Warbucks, Miss Farrell, and President Roosevelt burst out laughing. 'Thatta girl!' cried Mr Warbucks. 'Who the heck are Ralph and Shirley Mudge?'

'The birth certificate could easily enough have been forged,' Miss Farrell pointed out. 'But the odd thing is, they knew about the locket.'

'The locket – that's your key,' said President Roosevelt.

'But nobody knew about the locket except us,' said Mr Warbucks, puzzled. 'And the FBI, of course.'

'And Miss Hannigan,' remembered Annie.

Mr Warbucks and Miss Farrell, a comes-the-dawn look in their eyes, exchanged knowing nods. '*And* Miss Hannigan!' they chorused.

'*And* Miss Hannigan!' cried President Roosevelt.

Drake presented himself in the archway leading from the front foyer. 'Miss Hannigan, sir,' he announced, 'and the children from the orphanage, here for the Christmas party.' And into the room now marched Miss Hannigan at the head of her ragamuffin band of orphans. The orphans, wide-eyed with delight upon seeing the Christmas tree, the gifts, and Annie, rushed up to their old pal as they shouted, 'Annie, Annie Annie!' The first of the orphans to reach Annie was little Molly, who threw herself into Annie's arms and gave her a great big Christmas hug. And then the orphans ran to look at the gifts under the tree. 'Help yourselves, children,' said Miss Farrell, switching on the Christmas-tree lights, 'they're all for you.'

'Hooray!' shouted the orphans.

'Gee, Annie, what a great place this is,' said Kate as she picked out a pair of ice skates for herself from under the tree.

'Ahh, ugh, who'd want to live in this dump?' said Pepper, choosing a red bicycle for herself.

'Yeah, dump,' agreed Duffy, getting on to a hobbyhorse.

'Look, kids, there's about a dozen dolls for each of us!' shouted July.

'Oh, my goodness!' shrieked Tessie.

Meanwhile, Mr Warbucks was being nothing if not polite to Miss Hannigan, even though he knew how cruel she'd been to Annie, and even though he also now strongly suspected that she was involved with the couple calling themselves Ralph and Shirley Mudge. 'Ah, Miss Hannigan,' said Mr Warbucks, shaking her hand, 'I'm delighted to meet you. I've heard so much about you.'

'Same here,' replied Miss Hannigan. 'And I'd know you anywheres. You're *the* Oliver Warbucks, right?'

'Yes,' said Mr Warbucks. 'Now, let me introduce you to everyone. You already know my secretary, Miss Farrell, of course, and this is Drake, my butler, and that man over there is the President of the United States.'

'Yes, of course, I'm very delighted . . .' Miss Hannigan started to say, but then her jaw dropped open and her eyes glazed over in utter disbelief. 'Oh, my God President Roosevelt,' she stammered, collapsing into a chair, 'I'm in the same room with President Roosevelt.'

Drake came hurrying from the front door with an envelope. 'Mr Warbucks,' he whispered urgently, 'this has just come from the FBI.'

'Good,' said Mr Warbucks, tearing open the envelope and taking out a memorandum from J. Edgar Hoover. 'In Washington files,' the memorandum read, 'have turned up dossiers on a pair of swindlers who frequently identify themselves to their victims as Ralph and Shirley Mudge. From a study of our photographic files by Mudge victims we have now positively identified the pair as Daniel Francis 'Rooster' Hannigan and Muriel Jane Gumper, alias Lily St Regis, both of whom are wanted for federal crimes of fraud. If they return this

181

morning, please instruct my agents stationed in your house to take them immediately into custody.'

Mr Warbacks smiled as he handed the memorandum to Miss Farrell. 'Of course, now I remember that it was the man who did an imitation of a rooster in the front hallway of the orphanage who said "Oops, pardon me, blondie," whispered Miss Farrell. 'Who else but "Rooster" Hannigan?'

'Leapin' lizards!' cried Annie when Miss Farrell showed her the memorandum. 'Who woulda guessed it?'

Once again, Drake appeared in the archway. 'Sir, may I present Mr and Mrs Ralph Mudge,' he intoned, stepping aside to usher in Rooster and Lily in the disguises as the Mudges.

'Good morning,' Rooster croaked cheerfully. 'Merry Christmas, one and all!'

'Merry Christmas!' everyone replied.

'Ah, there she is, Shirley, our little girl,' said Rooster in a syrupy voice, pointing at Annie.

'Your little girl,' repeated Mr Warbucks with a smile.

'Hi, Mum, hi Dad,' Annie chirped.

'Well, we don't want to be no bother to nobody, on Christmas and all,' Rooster whined obsequiously. 'We just come to pick up Annie, her things, and, oh, yeah, the cheque.'

'Ah, yes, of course, the cheque,' said Mr Warbucks with a wink at Annie. 'I wouldn't want you to forget your cheque.' Mr Warbucks took the cheque from his pocket and held it out to Rooster. 'Here it is, Mr Mudge. Fifty thousand dollars. Certified.'

Rooster quickly grabbed the cheque and began to

tuck it into his wallet. This time he wasn't going to let it get away from him. 'Certified, huh?' asked Rooster, barely glancing at the cheque. 'Pay to the order of Ralph Mudge.'

'Oh, no, no, Mr Mudge, you'd better look at that cheque again,' said Mr Warbucks in a steely voice.

'Pay to the order of . . . "The jig is up"!' Rooster's jaw dropped open. He'd been found out!

'Yes, the jig is up, Daniel Francis Hannigan,' said Mr Warbucks sternly, 'also known as "Rooster" Hannigan, also known as Ralph Mudge.' He turned to Lily. 'And the jig is up for you, too, Miss Gumper.'

'Rooster, you dumb cluck, I could scratch your damn eyes out!' shrieked Lily.

'Drake,' commanded Mr Warbucks, 'summon in the FBI men from the anteroom.'

'I already have, sir,' said Drake politely, stepping aside to reveal a trio of brown-suited G-men who were holding drawn revolvers and pairs of handcuffs.

'Ah, good,' smiled Mr Warbucks. 'Would you arrest these two, please?'

'Yes, sir,' snapped the FBI agents, putting handcuffs on Rooster and Lily and starting to lead them away.

'Bye, Mum, bye, Dad,' Annie chirped.

Meanwhile, Miss Hannigan tiptoed up to the Christmas tree, surrounded herself with orphans, and began leading them in singing 'Silent Night'. Mr Warbucks strode up to Miss Hannigan, however, and placed a firm hand on her shoulder. 'And I believe that you'll find that this woman is their accomplice,' he said to the FBI agents. 'Arrest her, too, please.'

'Me? I didn't do nothin',' Miss Hannigan shrilly

protested. 'I never saw them two people before in my life.'

'Ahh, come off it, Aggie, you big liar!' shrieked Lily.

'Yeah, Sis, if Lily and me is goin' to jail for this one, so are you,' snarled Rooster. 'She was in on it, all right, give us all the dope about the locket and everything.'

Miss Hannigan turned to Mr Warbucks. 'Mr Warbucks, Oliver, I ain't never done nothin' to you,' she pleaded, 'I've always been a nice . . .'

'Madam,' President Roosevelt interrupted, 'the jig is up!'

Miss Hannigan looked about in panic and then spied Annie.'Annie, my little Annie,' she crooned, trying to sound like the sweetest lady in all the world, 'tell them how good and nice I always was to you.'

'Gee, I'm sorry, Miss Hannigan,' said Annie, backing warily away, 'but remember the one thing you always taught me: Never tell a lie!'

'Brat!' screeched Miss Hannigan. She tried to grab for Annie, but an FBI agent grabbed her first. 'I'm gonna let you in on a little secret,' she screamed, wriggling in the FBI agent's arms, 'I never liked you – you little gold digger!'

The FBI agent clamped handcuffs on Miss Hannigan's wrists. 'Come along with me,' he ordered.

'Get your crummy hands offa me!' she hollered, but soon she was gone, dragged off with Rooster and Lily to a federal lockup and almost certainly no less than ten years in jail. In Annie's life, in any event, that was the end of Miss Hannigan –she never saw her again.

'Annie,' said Mr Warbucks after the FBI men had gone with their prisoners, 'we'd like to meet your friends from the orphanage.'

Annie quickly assembled all the orphans – who'd been so busy playing with their Christmas toys under the tree that they hadn't seen what had happened to Miss Hannigan – and led them to Mr Warbucks and Miss Farrell.

'Kids,' said Annie, 'I'd like you to meet Miss Grace Farrell.'

'Hello,' chorused the orphans.

'Hi, kids,' Miss Farrell cheerfully replied.

'And that man over there is the President of the United States,' said Annie.

'Hello,' the orphans chorused again, totally un-impressed at meeting the President.

'Hi, kids!' cried President Roosevelt with a grin.

Annie took Mr Warbucks by the hand. 'And this,' she said, looking lovingly up at him, 'is . . . my father, Daddy Warbucks.'

'Hello,' chorused the orphans.

'Hi, kids,' said Mr Warbucks, hugging Annie close to him.

'And listen kids, I've great news,' Annie happily announced. 'Miss Hannigan is gone for good – to jail!'

'Hooray!' shouted the orphans.

'And you're not going to have to work at those sewing machines of yours ever again,' said Mr Warbucks. 'In fact, I'm going to see to it that every last one of you never spends another night in that damned orphanage! I'm going to see to it that you're all adopted by some very good friends of mine!'

'Hooray!' shouted the orphans.

'But, Molly, you're gonna live here with me and Mr

Warbucks, startin' right now,' said Annie to Molly, picking her up and hugging her. Little Molly began to laugh and to cry with joy at the same time.

'Just think of it, Molly, and all of you,' cried Annie, 'no more mush!'

'Hooray, hooray, hooray!' shouted the orphans for this was the best news of all.

Drake now ushered in a crowd of newly arrived guests – a group of fourteen elegantly dressed men and women. They must be some of Mr Warbucks' rich friends, thought Annie.

'Miss Annie's friends, sir,' announced Drake.

'*My* friends?' asked Annie. 'Golly, I don't know any . . .'

'You don't know me, Annie? Of course you do!' smiled a clean-shaven, aristoratic-looking man in an expensive grey pin-striped suit.

Annie suddenly realized who he was. 'Randy!' she cried, running up to him happily. And the beautiful woman with the upswept hairdo in the black silk Paris dress was none other than Sophie! Yes, the group was the whole gang from the Hooverville, who now crowded joyously around Annie to hug their old friend. Soon after Annie had told Mr Warbucks about her Hooverville pals and how kind they'd been to her, he'd arranged to have them released from jail and had given each of them a well-paying job in his New York headquarters. Moreover, he'd found them spacious Riverside Drive apartments and had them fitted out with superb wardrobes at his expense. But he'd saved the news of all this as a surprise for Annie on Christmas morning. Which it certainly was! Annie was bursting with joy at all of the good things that had so suddenly happened to her and her friends.

'Oh, Daddy,' she said to Mr Warbucks, 'you're so good to me – I couldn't have had a more perfect Christmas.'

'Gosh, I'm sorry to hear that,' said Mr Warbucks with a grin, 'because I've got one last gift for you.' He signalled to Drake, who motioned to a pair of uniformed footmen who were waiting out in the foyer. The footmen now entered the living room toting a huge square box done up in green wrapping paper with a big red ribbon tied around it.

'Here you are, Annie, your last Christmas present – I hope you like it,' smiled Mr Warbucks, leading her to the box. Annie had no idea what it could possibly be. Everyone gathered around.

'Come on, unwrap your dumb present,' said Pepper.

'Okay,' said Annie. She undid the ribbon, tore off the wrapping paper, lifted the top from the box, and there inside was . . . Sandy!

'Sandy!' shouted Annie exultantly. 'My Sandy!' The dog leapt out of the box and all but knocked Annie down as he put his big paws up on her shoulders and licked her face with joy. Annie hugged him and kissed him over and over again. Sandy! Mr Warbucks had found Sandy for her. 'Oh, Daddy!' cried Annie. 'Now my Christmas is really perfect.'

'Yes, I think maybe it is,' beamed Mr Warbucks, gazing down on the happy child and her equally happy dog. Miss Farrell stood grinning next to him. He took her hand and warmly squeezed it. Miss Farrell's heart leapt up, for, of course, she loved Oliver Warbucks as much as Annie did. Kneeling on the floor with her arms around Sandy's neck, Annie saw that Mr Warbucks and Miss Farrell were holding hands. Gee, thought Annie, maybe someday they'll get married and I'll have a mother, too. 'Wow,' breathed Annie, 'I think I'm happy.'

Outside, the snow had stopped and a bright sun had come out, shining down on Fifth Avenue, glistening on the new-fallen snow. The sunlight gleamed in the windows of the Warbucks living room, and Annie ran with Sandy to look out on the glittering, snow-covered fairyland scene. 'Look, Sandy,' Annie said, hugging the dog to her, 'tomorrow is here.'